Flurry the Bear

The Book of Snow

J.S. Skye

Flurry the Bear

The Book of Snow

2nd Edition – January 2015
First Published – February 2014

The Book of Snow
(Flurry the Bear – Book 4)
Copyright © 2015 J.S. Skye
All rights reserved.
www.FlurryTheBear.com

Cover art by Luís Figueiredo, J.S. Skye, & Tony Washington

ISBN: 069237308X
ISBN-13: 978-0692373088

CONTENTS

CHAPTER 1
NIGHTMARES

Fog – so thick that the white, furry bear was unable to see beyond his snout. The little cub, with his blue scarf, struggled through the mist. He groped to find his way through the haze. *There! I see a light up ahead!* he thought to himself. The bear cub approached the light source. He could make out what appeared to be an old oak table with four chairs around it – one at each side. The wooden tabletop was dressed and set with all of the trimmings for a feast. The cub licked his lips at the savory delights displayed in front of him. He rushed up to the table, climbed up on a chair, and reached for the food.

He grabbed a leg of roasted chicken from the plate and prepared to devour it. "Yum! Yum!" the cub exclaimed. He was about to take a bite, but before he could tear into the hunk of meat, a bone-chilling voice interrupted him.

"And what do you think you're doing?" asked the calm yet unnerving voice.

The bear froze in place. "I'm just eating. I'm hungry," he said. When he looked back down at his drumstick it was gone. All of the food had vanished. Not even the table or anything else existed any longer. The fog remained. Footsteps approached from behind. He spun around and saw a red panda with an evil grin and three scars down his right eye. The ominous figure wore a black jacket that went down to his ankles and had a sword at his side.

The teddy bear cub was terrified. The red panda came closer, and pulled his sword free of its scabbard. He drew back to swing his blade at the bear cub.

"You think it's over? I'm not finished yet! It's now your turn to perish!" The blade sliced down upon the cub. Flurry screamed and shot up out of bed. He panted heavily. Sweat poured down his fur.

"It was just a dream. Only a dream," Flurry whispered to himself. He wiped his face on his blanket while he tried to catch his breath. He gasped and looked about the dark room.

His plush brothers slept soundly. He

could hear them snore in their beds next to him. Then came the sound of footsteps approaching the bedroom door. Flurry raised his blanket to his nose in fear.

The door opened. Flurry sighed with relief. A young lady stood in the open doorway. The oriental female had long, straight black hair and glasses. Still half asleep herself, she stood there in her nightshirt and yawned. "Flurry! Are you all right?" she asked.

The poor little bear cried. He managed to get a couple of sentences out. "Yes, Mommy. It was only a bad dream."

The cub's mother immediately rushed to Flurry's bedside and scooped him up in her arms. "Awww! There, there. Everything's going to be fine. I'm with you. Hush now, you're safe with me."

Lynn cradled her furry boy. He clung tightly to her neck. Flurry shivered and sobbed while she stroked his fur. "Come with me. I'll make you a warm glass of milk. It'll help you relax," she told the cub.

"Can I have chocolate in it?" Flurry inquired.

"Yes, of course you can! Anything for my little boy," she assured him. Lynn carried Flurry out of the bedroom, and quietly shut the door behind her. She brought the little fellow to the kitchen and set him on the countertop. "So, do you want to tell me what that was all about?"

"It's nothing," he answered.

"Flurry, I wasn't born yesterday. You've barely spoken about your trip back to your home at the North Pole. That was more than two months ago. You were so excited to go, but when you came back you had nothing to say about it. Now you have nightmares every night, and you keep screaming the name 'Jack' in your sleep. As your mother, I think I deserve an explanation."

Flurry peered down at the floor. He did not want to share any of the details with his mother. He was afraid of what she would think if she knew about his adventures.

"Fine, I'll make you a deal. You can tell me just little bits, if you want. We can work this out together. Every little bit you want to tell me, you'll get a special prize."

"Really?" the bear's face lit up. "Like a cookie or ice cream?"

"Sure," she replied.

"Well, a lot of things happened when I went back to Ursus."

"Ursus?" Flurry's mother seemed

surprised. "I've never heard of this place."

"I mean back home. Ursus is the name of the village I come from."

"Oh! You've never told me that before."

"Does that count toward a cookie, too? I hope I get a treat for that!"

The cub's mother shook her head and chuckled. "Just go on."

"Well, when I was there, I found out that my mama and papa had replaced me." He paused and decided to rephrase his statement. "Well, they didn't really replace me, but now I have a sister that I didn't have before."

"Flurry! You never told me that you have a sister! That's so wonderful!"

"Yeah, I didn't think so at the time. I was really hurt, so I ran away from home. Then my sister found a map stuck to Caboose, and the three of us decided to follow the map. I thought it led to a land of pies, but the map led us into danger. We met some really bad wolves. The wolves tried to trick me into stealing from some grumpy cats, but I didn't do it. Then after that …"

"Wait a minute!" Flurry's mother was overwhelmed at the speed Flurry conveyed the information to her. She quickly interjected. "You're going really fast, and I'm sure you're skipping over details. Why don't you slow down and start from the beginning? We have time."

So Flurry spent the next hour recalling his adventures. He began with the land of the Sourpie and moved on to the story about how he reunited the two kings, foiled the plans of the evil wolves, accidentally set Jack Frost free, met Chingu the Protector, and then the story of Drizzle's sacrifice to save the entire world from evil. It was a lot to tell, and Flurry's mother was shocked beyond words. She had previously known nothing about any of this. For better or for worse, Flurry had kept it all a secret – which was amazing for him, since he rarely could keep his mouth shut about anything.

Flurry's mother could hardly believe her ears. On top of that, she did not know if she should be proud of him for being so brave and helping others or scold him for putting himself and others at risk. She looked at his face, and her heart melted. She knew that Flurry had been through so much, far more than any child should ever have to go through.

Flurry finished his third beverage for the night. He wiped away his chocolate milk-mustache and raised his arms for a hug. His mother obliged, and carried him to her bedroom. "Tonight you can sleep in our bed. You'll be safe here. Tomorrow we'll all go out and do something special." Flurry smiled and clapped his paws excitedly.

Flurry snuggled up to his mother. There was plenty of room on the bed between his mother and father, but Flurry was fearful that Jack Frost might get him in his sleep, so he cuddled up close to his mother for protection. They each fell fast asleep while she stroked the fur on her adopted bear cub's arm.

Flurry's teddy bear parents still lived up in the land of Mezarim. Flurry always referred to them as Mama and Papa. Six months ago, Flurry had been ordered to live with a human couple in the country of

Middleasia to learn a lesson in humility. It was a form of discipline for his prideful attitude and behavior. Flurry always referred to his human parents as Mommy and Daddy to differentiate them from his teddy bear mama and papa back in Ursus.

The next morning, Flurry woke up, rubbed his eyes, and yawned. While he stretched, he deduced that his father was at work. He knew his mother was in the kitchen, since the bed was empty, and he could hear the rattling of pots and pans. Flurry wondered what time it was. The sunlight already shined brightly into the room. It was a fine summer's day.

Flurry hopped down from the very large bed and scurried to the partially-opened bedroom door. He peeked out from the room, and was met with his mother's greeting. "Good morning! I'm glad you're finally up! I was about to come in and wake you." Flurry's mother was all dressed and ready for the day. She wore blue jeans, leather boots, and a forest green tee-shirt.

"Are you ready for a surprise?" she asked.

"Uh huh!" Flurry vigorously nodded with affirmation.

"Okay, then, let's go! The other fuzzies are already in the car. I wanted to let you sleep for a little while longer before we left. Today, we're going to the park."

"Yay!" Flurry shouted. His countenance greatly improved. In addition to the good news, he felt better to have gotten such a heavy burden off of his chest the night before. It was also the first good night of sleep he had experienced in what seemed like ages. On this fine day, Flurry felt able enough to tackle the whole world.

He joined his brothers in the family car. Everyone was strapped in with seatbelts – though it was unlikely that the cubs would be hurt if they were ever in a car accident. Being a plush animal had its advantages.

The fuzzies, which their human parents liked to collectively call them, were so small that they all fit across the back seat together. Flurry sat on the far left followed by a tall, slender lion with golden fur named Noah. Next was a cream-colored polar bear named Caboose, and then came a very small lion with light-brown fur, a big bushy mane, and reading glasses. The little lion's name was Boaz. Last, but not least, was a little brown bunny rabbit named Honja. Honja looked quite enthusiastic for once. He was typically grumpy, so this particular day was off to a great start.

Upon their arrival at the park, the little ones did not waste any time. They rushed out to play. Their mother smiled as she watched them play together.

The park had many things for them to enjoy. There was a vast array of slides, seesaws, jungle gyms, and swing sets. However, the fuzzies were the most interested in the little tree house at the far end of the park grounds.

As the day progressed, it became quite humid, and the sun baked everything in sight. For this reason, no children were at the park. The heat did not bother the fuzzies since they did not sweat – well, none of them but Flurry. Flurry was a unique creation, and the typical rules did not always apply to him. Ever since Christopher

Kringle brought Flurry to life, he had been special in more ways than one.

Honja resided in the tree house and looked down from above. More true to form, he was irritated with his brothers below.

Noah stood in the grass with a long, slender branch in his paw. Flurry held a branch of his own. His had a smaller twig tied on with a vine to make a paw guard, as though it were a sword. Flurry also wore a picnic blanket tied around his neck like a cape.

Caboose stood across from the other plush animals in opposition to them. He was right under the tree house Honja occupied. He wore a plastic bowl on his head, which had previously been filled with potato chips. He also had a stick which he held in his mouth. Boaz was draped with a black plastic trash bag. He had an indignant expression on his face. He stood next to Flurry and glared at him.

Their mother watched from a distance. She tried to figure out what kind of a game Flurry had concocted.

"What do I do?" Caboose asked.

"For the last time! You're one of the evil polar bears! You're supposed to protect Jack from us," Flurry replied. His frustration was apparent to all.

Noah simply shook his head, and Boaz sighed.

"Who's Jack?" Caboose replied.

"Oh, my goodness! Caboose! I already told you!" Flurry shouted. "Okay! Time out, everyone! Time out, while I explain this to Caboose … again."

The others were relieved to have a break.

Boaz and Noah rushed over to the tree house for some shade from the sun. They did not have sweat glands, but the sun was scorching hot, nonetheless.

"Caboose! Remember? Honja is pretending to be Jack. Jack is evil. You're one of Jack's polar bears. Boaz is Drizzle. Noah and I are ourselves. Okay?"

"Uh, huh!" Caboose nodded his head.

"Great! Come on guys! We have to save the day and stop Jack's evil plan!" Flurry held up his branch high in the air to rally the troops.

The two lions reluctantly moseyed over to him. Honja remained up in the tree house with his arms crossed. He looked more frustrated than ever.

"Attack!" Flurry shouted. The three little warriors ran toward Caboose and the tree house. Caboose looked to and fro, turned around, and ran toward the tree house, too. "No!" Flurry bellowed. He came to an abrupt stop without warning. Noah and Boaz crashed into him. After their brief fumble, Flurry got back up, brushed the dirt off of his fur, and approached the polar bear. "Caboose, you aren't supposed to run away! You have to stop us from attacking Jack."

"Who's Jack?" Caboose asked.

Flurry immediately buried his face in his paws and shook his head. The way things were going, it would be a very long day. Boaz and Noah were delighted when their mother opened the cooler and brought out more refreshments. "Drinks! Come and get them!" she called out to them.

"Yay!" they shouted, tossed their props down, and ran to get a beverage.

Honja, who remained in the tree house, looked perplexed and muttered angrily to himself. He shouted down to his brothers, but nobody responded. Honja had originally been purchased from a shop in another country. He was able to understand English just fine, but was unable to speak it. Luckily, Boaz had taken it upon himself to learn Honja's language, so that he could speak with and understand the rabbit. Their mother and father could also speak Honja's language. Honja had some individuals he could communicate with, if he chose to.

When the rabbit saw that his friends did not acknowledge him, he muttered to himself angrily and climbed down from the tree to go join them.

As Honja was about to arrive at the table, Flurry ran past him, back out toward the tree house again. The bear shouted, "Come on, guys! We have a land to save!"

"Awww! Come on, Flurry! We don't want to play anymore! Let's do something different," Boaz groaned. He loved Flurry like a brother, but Flurry often got on everyone's nerves – well, everyone except for Caboose. Nothing ever appeared to bother the polar bear cub. No matter what Flurry did, Caboose always looked up to and admired him – which was why Caboose was the only one that ran back out with Flurry. The other three siblings stayed behind.

"What? Why don't you want to play?" Flurry asked. He was genuinely perplexed by the others' reluctance. Flurry had come a long way since he arrived in Middleasia, nearly six months ago, but he still had a serious pride problem. He just could not see past himself at times.

"I believe I speak for the rest of us when I say that we're tired of always playing the same game, and tired of you always getting to be the hero."

Noah and Honja nodded their heads in agreement. Caboose had a dumbfounded look on his face. He decided to nod his head in agreement, because that was what everyone else was doing.

"You, too, Caboose?" Flurry was shocked. "Fine! I'll play by myself!" Flurry stormed off. He swung his branch violently at the grass as he stomped toward the tree house. Caboose trailed along behind him, like a lost puppy.

"Actually, why don't all of you take a break? It's hot out, and all of you could use some down time," their mother suggested.

"That's okay. They can go. I'll stay out here," Flurry answered.

"No! I wasn't asking," his mother replied. She removed her black-framed glasses, sighed, and rubbed her eyes. The heat was getting to her, but she felt irritated with Flurry, too. She then continued. "It's not an option. In the car!"

"But, Mommy!"

"Don't 'but, Mommy' me! Get in the car! Now!"

Flurry's mother wore an expression that communicated she meant business. She pointed toward the vehicle with an angry scowl. Flurry grumbled and stomped back toward their transportation. He tossed his branch in the grass and ripped off his makeshift cape.

Flurry's mother often did not know what

to do with him. He was a very stubborn bear. However, she could not help but feel sympathy for him. He had been exposed to so much more than most adults have ever gone through in their entire life, and she had no idea how to help him. She could not take him to a counselor either. How would she explain the existence of a living, breathing teddy bear? Even taking her boys out to the park was a risk, but on a day like this, nobody else was out.

The cubs were excited to finally arrive home. Inside, it was nice and cool from the air conditioner. Noah went over to the couch. He climbed up, opened one of his sketchbooks, and drew in it.

Caboose noticed that a butterfly had slipped in while the door was open, so he ran off to chase it. He was completely mesmerized by the most unsuspecting things. Caboose was always so curious about everything, and no matter how many times you told him something, it would always be the first time he had ever heard about it.

Boaz went into the bedroom and fiddled with his laptop, and Honja snuck off and hid in a corner with his headset to listen to his tunes.

Flurry, on the other hand, was in a very foul mood. He continued to pout while he paced back and forth. He needed to make it clear to his mother that he was angry at her for ruining his fun at the park.

"Flurry, I know what you're doing. If you keep acting like that, you can go to bed. Do you want that?" she asked.

Flurry did not want to answer her. He just

stood there with his arms interlocked. He glared at her with an angry face.

"Okay! Have it your way! To bed, now!"

"Awww!" Flurry whined. His expression was answered with an cross stare from his mother. She pointed toward the bedroom with an exaggerated gesture. The little cub stormed off to his room and would have slammed the door, if he had been strong enough to do so with one that was human-sized.

Instead, he stomped over to his bead. He ripped his bedspread away, crawled up into his bed, and yanked the blanket over his head. He often liked to hide under the covers when he wanted to pretend that the world outside did not exist anymore.

Flurry huddled under his blanket and wallowed in self-pity. He had no idea what to do about his life anymore. At heart, he was still a child, but the things he experienced had now changed him. Grief overtook him. He thought about how he went from having exciting adventures to being scolded by his mother.

Bedtime for the others eventually came. Their mother tucked them all in and gave them each a kiss on the cheek. When she came to Flurry's bed, she had a bit of a tug-of-war with him to get his blanket away. "You don't want your bedtime kiss?" she asked.

Flurry sat there with his arms folded and his brow furrowed. "Well, you get one, whether you like it or not." She quickly snagged him by the arm and gave him a big smooch on his adorable little face.

"Mommy!" Flurry shouted and wiped his

cheek.

"Good night, everyone. I love all of you very much!"

They each replied in their own manner. Noah drew a heart on his sketchpad and held it up for her to view. Boaz and Caboose returned the sentiment. Honja replied in his native tongue. Flurry, however, did not answer her at all. He wanted her to know how angry he was. As far as he was concerned, she had ruined his entire day.

Their mother switched off the light and shut the door.

"You know, that was pretty rude of you!" Boaz informed the moody bear.

"Whatever! I don't want to talk to you or anyone else right now," Flurry answered. He laid his head on the pillow, pulled his blanket close, and closed his eyes. What seemed like hours went by at the pace of a crawl. Flurry tossed and turned, but sleep eluded him. He did not know why he could not rest. Flurry was uncertain if his lack of rest was due to his fear of nightmares, or if it was guilt for the way he had treated his mother. The cub knew he was wrong to be mean to her.

Flurry thought, *Maybe if I make things right I can get some sleep.* So he pulled away the blanket and sat up. He quickly climbed down, went to his dresser, and brought out a piece of paper and some crayons. He thought that drawing a picture for his mother would be a thoughtful way to say that he was sorry.

Flurry felt a bit better about himself as he thought about the gift he was going to make for his mother. He opened another drawer, where he was about to grab a light, when something dawned on him. He realized he had forgotten all about the gift Christopher Kringle had sent home with him close to two months ago. It was not like him to forget about a gift. All of the excitement to be home and with his friends had caused it to slip his mind. After he put it under his bed so long ago, it was a case of out of sight, out of mind.

Flurry loudly rummaged around under his bed. The noise roused Boaz from his sleep. "What are you up to now?" Boaz grumbled.

"Oh, my! I can't believe that I forgot about Santa's gift!" was Flurry's explanation from the darkness in his corner of the room.

"Ah ha!" Flurry exclaimed. He pulled out a package wrapped in drab brown paper and tied with string. He ripped the paper off to reveal an old, dusty book with a locked clasp. The hardbound text had decorative metals and precious stones laid into its cover. Most peculiarly, the center of the cover had an indentation that was empty. It appeared to Flurry that something belonged there, but had been taken out.

Flurry took note how the metal and gemstones were placed in such a way that they resembled his family crest.

A folded slip of paper stuck out from the book's pages. Flurry removed it and opened it up, but he was unable to read it. He handed it to Boaz, who was now out of bed and had come to Flurry's side.

"What does it say?" Flurry asked.

Boaz put on his glasses. "This side says, *The Book of Snow*," he answered. The lion cub flipped the folded paper open and read aloud: "I believe this belongs to you. Signed, C.K."

"Hmmm." Flurry was very curious. Just at that moment a glow came from the drawer of his nightstand. Flurry got up, opened the drawer, and grabbed the crystal he had stashed away there. It shone brightly. Right before their eyes, the beautiful gem changed shape in Flurry's paw.

"Look! It's the size of that hole in the book!" exclaimed Boaz. The lion directed Flurry's attention to the book's cover.

Being curious, Flurry placed the stone into the open hole. Immediately the book's clasp unhinged, and it sprang open. Blue light beamed out from the pages of the book.

At this point, the others were now awake. Noah and Caboose rubbed their eyes. Honja rushed out from his bed to put a stop to whatever Flurry was doing. He was exhausted, and it enraged him that Flurry always had to be doing something to keep him from his rest.

Flurry reached out to touch the book, but Boaz warned him. "Wait! Are you sure that's safe?"

Flurry drew back momentarily and thought about the question. "I'm not sure, but I don't think Santa would give me something dangerous."

"Good point," Boaz reasoned.

Flurry reached out and turned a page in the book. He examined the pages. Each piece of parchment was decorated with beautiful drawings. "My kind of book!" Flurry exclaimed. "I like books that have pictures."

"Flurry, is that you?" came a muffled voice from outside the bedroom door.

"Oh no! Mommy heard me!" Flurry whispered to Boaz.

"Flurry, you had better be in bed by the time I reach the door." The sound of Flurry's doom approached.

"Quick! We have to hide the book!" Flurry whispered to Boaz.

As Flurry was about to close the book, Honja arrived. He was beyond irritated with his white-furred roommate. Flurry reached over and patted Honja on the head while he closed the book with his other paw. Instantly, Flurry and Honja were sucked into the book, the cover slammed shut, and the clasp locked back in place.

Boaz, Caboose, and Noah were dumbfounded. They stared at the tome, and then at each other. None of the cubs knew what to do.

The sound of footsteps drew nearer. Noah pushed the book under Flurry's bed and pulled Flurry's blanket up over his pillow. Boaz did likewise with Honja's bed. The three of them all jumped back into their beds and pretended to be asleep.

The door creaked open, and their mother peeked into the room. They seemed to all be asleep, so she turned back, and the door latched shut again. The sound of footsteps grew fainter until they could not hear her anymore. At the distant sound of their mother's bedroom door closing, Boaz let out a sigh of relief.

The three cubs sat back up from their beds and looked at each other. Boaz glanced toward Noah and asked, "What are we going to do? Flurry and Honja are inside the book!" Boaz had a look of sheer terror on his face. Noah shrugged. Caboose had already gotten out of bed and now sniffed at the book. The polar bear dragged it back out from under Flurry's bed.

"Maybe we should open it and see if say are in sare," lisped Caboose.

"No way! What if we open it, and we get sucked in, too?" Boaz replied. "I don't know how we're going to break the news to Mommy. We need to talk to the person Flurry calls Santa. Maybe he'll know what to do."

CHAPTER 2
NERO

The chirps of crickets were the loudest sound to be heard in the quiet, peaceful village located in a very distant land known as Kunteris. This region was far beyond the reaches of Christopher Kringle's domain or any land that had even heard of him.

It was a fine summer evening. Only the occasional hoot of an owl broke the continuous drone of nocturnal insects. The wind was soft and refreshing against the tapestry of green foliage. The trees swayed with each subtle wisp of the breeze. Their twin images reflected in the moonlit surface of a still, gentle pond.

Aside from the full moon, nothing but the dwindling embers of a central campfire lit the encampment of bamboo huts with grass roofs. The windows were almost completely dark except for one; a slight glow came from a larger hut on the outskirts of the village.

Inside stood a gray, furry animal with black stripes on her tail. Her snout was long and slender, and she had black fur that encircled each eye. She wore a pair of goggles while she chipped away at a gemstone on the table. The hut had been converted into a humble little workshop. There were metal gears which lay all over the place. A stone grinder, a box full of various gems, and a variety of tools littered the tables and shelves. There were a number of contraptions that looked like steam-powered mechanical inventions of some kind. By all appearances, this little worker was quite savvy with mechanical things.

The night grew late for her. She was deeply fatigued. It might have been more evident if she did not already have dark circles around her eyes naturally. Her work was very dear to her heart, and it always came before sleep or anything else. This project was of the utmost importance, and she was so close to being done with it. All she had to do was finish the gemstone and place it in the book, which she had yet to give a title.

She chipped away at the crystal. Her mind focused on how difficult it had been to get her paws on such a rare item. The stone was said to have special properties over space and time, and it cost her a pretty penny to acquire.

The chipping, grinding, and polishing finally came to a halt. She held up the stone against the moonlight that shone down through a skylight in the hut's roof.

"Perfect!" the female coon said to herself. "Now, let's see if you'll fit." She carefully laid the gemstone into an indentation on the book's cover. It dropped into place smoothly. She was well pleased with her finished product. The raccoon realized the job would have been much more difficult if not for having found a way of depleting the crystal of its power temporarily. The precious stone was an unlimited, self-sustaining energy source, and it would have been problematic to work with it in that state. She had used her vast knowledge and devised a way to short out the gemstone long enough for her to mold it to her desired configuration. If she had not done this, the crystal would not have been able to be shaped. It would have adapted and changed to any form it so desired. It was like it had a mind of its own.

The indentation in the book's cover worked to confine the gemstone to one size, as long as it remained in the book. "Now all I need to do is activate this little fella, and it'll be done," the raccoon told herself. A pleased smile came to her adorable, furry face.

She pulled out a smaller gemstone. It radiated blue light, shining brighter than the stars in the sky. She touched the smaller gemstone to the larger stone inlaid in the book's cover. The light transferred from the small stone to the larger one that was now part of the book.

The book was complete. Its centerpiece gleamed brightly. She smiled at her masterful craftsmanship. Before she had a chance to take it all in, the locked clasp came free. The book sprang open, and two furry objects flew out from the book's pages and across the room.

"Ahhh!" Flurry bellowed through the air before he landed in a pile of hay. He sat up and rubbed his head. "Wow! What a trip! I wonder where I am," Flurry asked himself out loud. He looked himself over and brushed hay off of his fur.

Suddenly, Flurry sensed something move beneath him. He jumped up and spun around. In the hay below was Honja, and the little rabbit did not look pleased with Flurry for having landed on him.

"Oh! Hi, Honja! You're here, too! Yay!" Flurry reached out to pat Honja on the head, but Honja quickly shot back into the pile of hay to avoid Flurry's touch. The rabbit hated being petted on the head. No matter how many times Flurry had been reminded, it never stuck in his memory.

"Honja? Honja, you can come out now. I won't pet you, I promise."

Flurry and Honja had not realized they were not the only ones in the room. The raccoon cleared her throat, which startled Flurry. With a gasp, he whirled around to face the source of the sound. Flurry was relieved that it was a cute raccoon and not something more sinister.

The raccoon cautiously waved to him, as

if she had no idea what else to do. She had not expected the book to fly open, let alone bring visitors.

"Oh! Hello, I'm Flurry!" said the little cub.

Honja peeked out from the hay and then went back into hiding. "Hi, there. I'm Lotora. Who's your little friend?" the raccoon responded.

"Oh, him? That's Honja."

"He's a cute little mouse!"

"Oh no! He hates that!"

Honja was infuriated. He ran out from under the pile of hay and head-butted the raccoon in the foot. He then did likewise to Flurry before he leapt back into his hiding spot.

"Oh, my! I'm so sorry! Please don't be mad at him. He has a bit of a temper. That was very rude of him."

"It's fine," Lotora reassured him.

"You see, he's a bunny rabbit. He doesn't like to be touched, petted on the head, or mistaken for a mouse. He probably has an entire list of things he hates, but those are the ones I remember at the moment." Flurry put his paw to his mouth and pondered if he had left any out or not.

Lotora knelt down and leaned toward the haystack. She spoke softly, saying, "I'm sorry, little one. Please come out. I didn't mean to upset you." She tried to coerce the little brown bunny out of his seclusion. "I have a carrot for you, if you'll come out. I'm not planning on eating it." She stood up and reached for a plate of food that sat on the table next to her book. Some of the food had only been half eaten. It looked like she had barely nibbled any of it.

Lotora dangled the carrot down low where Honja could reach it. He peeked out from the hay. Slowly, he inched his way out with his ears swooped back. He sniffed at the carrot, grabbed it, and darted back inside the hay.

"Honja! You didn't even say thank you! Mommy would be so disappointed!"

"*Kamsahamnida,*" came a faint voice from within the hay.

"*Nae*," the raccoon replied.

"Wait a minute! You can understand him?" Flurry was surprised.

"Of course, I can."

"Wow!"

"So, where are you two from?" Lotora was fascinated by her new guests.

"Well, I'm from a village called Ursus.

Maybe you've heard of it?"

"No, I can't say that I have."

"How could you not know about Ursus? That's where Santa's lives!"

"Who's Santa?"

"You don't know who Santa is? Oh my goodness!" Flurry was shocked beyond belief.

"I'm sorry, but no," Lotora replied. "What about him?" she asked while she pointed to where Honja still hid. "Is he from Ursus, too?"

"No. I think Daddy bought him in some distant country, on his way back to Middleasia," Flurry replied.

"Where's Middleasia?"

"You don't know where Middleasia is either?"

"No," Lotora replied. "Can you point to it

on a map?"

"I suppose," Flurry replied. He climbed up onto a chair to get a view of the table top.

Lotora pulled out a map from her shelf, blew off the dust, and unrolled it across the table. She lifted Flurry up from the chair and set him on the table next to the map.

On all fours, Flurry crawled over to one corner of the map and examined it. "Hmmm. It should be right around … hey! I don't recognize anything on this map. This doesn't look anything like the maps at Mommy and Daddy's house. It doesn't look like my Uncle Vinegar's maps either. Where am I?"

"You're in the land of Kunteris. This village is named Coonlei."

"Kunteris? Kunteris? Where in the world is Kunteris? I've never even heard of

Kunteris before!" Flurry looked worried and flustered. He started to breathe heavily.

"Calm down! Relax! Everything is fine. Just breathe. I have a theory why you don't recognize anything."

Flurry calmed down a bit. He nervously stuffed Lotora's leftovers in his mouth to cope. A smile came upon Lotora's face. Her entire demeanor changed. She acted excited about her internal thoughts. "Aha! This is amazing! If my theory is true, this is the greatest news ever! What were you doing the moment before you arrived here?"

With food stuffed in his mouth, he replied, "I was looking at a book that Santa gave me. It's called *The Book of Snow*. I put a crystal in it, and it opened up. I turned some pages, and the next thing I know, I'm here."

"*The Book of Snow*, huh?" Lotora turned and paced back and forth. She chanted the phrase "*The Book of Snow*" repeatedly under her breath. To Flurry, it looked like she was having a discreet conversation with herself.

Her muttering reminded the bear cub of his uncle. Uncle Vinegar often did likewise, when Flurry observed him deep in his studies. "What? What is it?" Flurry inquired.

"Well, my theory is that you've traveled in time through my book. I deduce you're from the future, because I haven't named the book yet. I was thinking of calling it *The Book of Frost*. I made this book to be a recounting of the horrors and tyranny brought upon our many lands and nations by Jack Frost. This book is to be a record of all that was, is, and will be.

"With each day, his strength grows. He's

been killing off all of the red pandas so he can be the one and only in all of existence. He doesn't want to have any rival to his beauty or power. The number of red pandas that still live are few, and those that remain have been in hiding for many years."

"Wait a minute! Jack's alive? But I saw him die!"

Lotora's tone instantly became grave. "Hush! Do you want to be heard by one of his spies? Don't say things like that! You can be put to death if the wrong soul heard you say that."

"Say what?" Flurry was confused.

"To say that Jack's dead. He's very much alive and ruling from his palace at Ursidea."

"Finally! A name I know! That place is very close to Ursus, where I'm from."

"Wait a minute! Now I know where

you're from. The land of Mezarim, right?"

"That's what I said earlier!" Flurry was suddenly frustrated that he had to repeat himself.

"No, you said Ursus," Lotora corrected the little cub.

"Well, same difference," Flurry returned.

"Can I assume there's another name for the one you call Santa?"

"Yeah, I suppose," Flurry replied with an embarrassed look on his face. "The other bears call him Mr. Kringle."

"Kringle!" Lotora gasped. She was shocked beyond words. "I had no idea you were speaking of Nikolas Kringle!"

"His name is Santa," answered the cub.

"Whether you call him Santa or not, Nikolas is renowned in this part of the world, though he isn't a very well-liked man. It's because of him that Jack exists. Many have sought his death. In fact, he'd probably be dead if he could be found. He's quite an elusive man. Most knowledge of him has become akin to legend or fairy tale. Good luck trying to find him!"

Flurry was not sure what she meant by the name Nikolas. He always heard his papa call him Chris. Flurry cried and buried his face in his paws. "What's going on? This isn't how it's supposed to be! This is wrong. It's all wrong! Where I'm from, everyone loves Santa, and Jack is dead. This is a nightmare!" Flurry smacked himself in the face and said, "Wake up, Flurry! Wake up! Wake up, Flurry! Wake up! This is just a dream! It's just a bad dream! Wake up!" It was no use; he was still there. Tears streamed down the cub's face.

Lotora's demeanor softened, and a tear came to her eye. She felt bad for making the poor cub cry. "There, there, little one. I'm sorry for being so stern. If what you say is true, then there is hope yet. I feared that Jack would rule forever and destroy everything that I hold dear. If you're from the future, as I suspect, then you're a herald of good news. You may become a beacon of hope to us all. Your presence means that the suffering of all of the lands will come to an end someday. Thank you!" She gave Flurry a warm hug.

The hug did not last long before screams were heard from beyond the walls of the hut. Lotora quickly let go of Flurry and rushed to the window.

"What is it?" Flurry asked.

"Oh no! Not them! They know! Quick!

We have to get out of here!" Lotora hurriedly grabbed Flurry from the table and set him back on his feet before she turned back to grab the book. Honja frightfully peeked out from the hay. He came out and trailed closely behind Flurry and Lotora. "Let's go! We must not be captured."

"Why? What is it?"

"Jack's henchmen are here. They're burning the huts. Somehow they must've found out that we've been hiding red pandas here. Quickly! Let's move!"

Lotora rushed out of the hut and darted toward the tree line as fast as she possibly could. Flurry and Honja followed. They made it into the brush just as something approached the hut. Right before Flurry's eyes stood a creature he had never seen before. He thought it was a fox at first, due to its orange fur and canine features, but it was far worse. Its paws looked like burning embers, and it had three tails. The tip of each tail and the creature's back were aflame. For some reason, the fire did not seem to hurt the beast. As the creature looked around with its searing orange eyes, Flurry shivered. It scoured the area for anyone or anything to be its next victim. With a sweep of its tail, the hut was set ablaze.

"No!" Lotora shouted. Flurry quickly put his paw over her mouth and muffled her objection.

"Shhhhh! You don't want it to hear us," Flurry whispered.

Flurry was too late. At the sound of Lotora's voice, the flaming, foxlike creature looked in their direction.

"Maybe it didn't notice us," Flurry tried to reassure Honja and himself. Honja shook with fear. He backed up slowly and pulled leaves down around himself.

The flaming beast came near to their location in the brush and sniffed around. It appeared to be aware of their presence. A growl came from the horrific creature. It took a step closer. Its snout was right next to Flurry's head, where he remained hidden on the far side of a tree.

It looked as if they would be eaten alive, until a loud and commanding voice called out from the midst of the flaming huts. "You there! Quit fooling around! We have more huts to burn!" The flaming fox immediately withdrew and ran back toward the voice.

"Phew!" Flurry let out a sigh of relief. As he wiped the sweat from his brow, he exclaimed, "That was close!"

Flurry turned to find Lotora curled up in a ball, sobbing.

"What's wrong?"

"It's over. It's all over. If Jack finds Tomodachi, our hope is lost. He's the only one who has been bold enough to speak out against Jack."

"Hey! I know that name! Doggy told me all about him. He beat Jack."

Lotora instantly looked up with a startled expression. "What? Are you sure?"

"Uh, huh," answered Flurry. He nodded his head vigorously.

"Then we have to try to save him! It's risky, but everything depends on his survival. Come quickly! I know where the other villagers were hiding him."

Lotora jumped to her feet, grabbed Flurry

by the paw, and ran toward the huts. "Come on, Honja!" Flurry shouted back to the bunny.

Honja shook his head in fear. He trembled so much that you would have thought he was freezing to death. Honja simply did not have the desire for adventure that Flurry did. He preferred the safety of his home and the quiet of his own little corner of the house. After all, he was just a little rabbit. He did not have the means to defend himself from something like that creature he saw.

Just then a growl was heard, and the bushes shifted. In fear, Honja ran and called out to Flurry, "*Gah-chi gah!*"

The three of them made their way across the village of huts, ducking down and hiding behind anything they could find. So far, so good; they had not been spotted yet. Flurry saw three of the flaming monsters led by another kind of fox, who appeared to be the leader. The one in command was an arctic fox with pearly-white fur. He stood upright on two legs like a man. Over his white fur he wore black pants, boots, a vest, and two swords, one at each side.

"Hurry up already! They have to be here somewhere!" shouted their commander. The arsonist walked over, grabbed the village leader from among the prisoners, and slammed him against the door of the nearest hut. "Tell me where he is, or I'll burn down your entire village!" The raccoon would not speak. The fox tossed the raccoon back to the ground. The arctic fox shouted, "Very well! Have it your way!" He whistled at the flaming beasts and commanded them, saying, "Finish the job! Burn down the entire village!" Screams resounded through the chaos that ensued.

"We have to do something, quickly! Tomodachi's hut is already on fire," Lotora insisted.

Flurry and Honja raced after Lotora. She came up to a hut almost completely engulfed in flames. She looked concerned when she peered in through a gap in the wall. "I don't see them. Tomodachi and Yujin should be in there," said the raccoon. She gave Flurry a troubled glance.

"Let me see." Flurry peeked in. "Where would they hide? The hut is so small."

"They would be underneath the floor. We dug out a hole to hide them in if trouble came."

"Maybe they're still inside and can't get out," Flurry proposed.

"Oh no! That's terrible! We can't even get in to check!" Lotora was frantic.

"No, but Honja can," Flurry replied. The bear shifted his gaze to his rabbit friend. The little bunny was taken off guard. His mouth dropped open, and he pointed at himself in disbelief. "*Nah?*" he asked.

"Yes, you! You can fit through the hole and make sure they aren't trapped."

Honja shook his head vigorously in rejection of the idea. There was no way Honja wanted to have any part in going into a burning hut.

"Come on! You'll be a hero!" Flurry attempted to appeal to his friend.

"Something needs to be done quickly, before the roof collapses!" shouted Lotora.

Honja relented. He rushed in through the hole and looked around. The smoke was so thick that nobody else could have been in there without being smothered to death from the lack of air. Luckily for Honja, he was so small and low to the ground that it allowed space for him to breathe. He looked all around. It seemed hopeless until he noticed the hidden door. The door was lashed shut. He chewed away at the leather rope the held it secure. Fire continued to rain down around him as he gnawed at the binding.

Outside, Flurry and Lotora were deeply troubled. They had neither seen nor heard anything from Honja. Flurry was uncertain if his friend was even alive.

"Honja!" Flurry and Lotora shouted together, but there was no answer.

"I hope he's okay," Lotora told her new friend.

"Me, too," said Flurry with a very worried

tone to his voice. Sweat rolled down his face. The situation was dire, and there was still no sign of the rabbit. Snapping, crackling, and tearing could be heard as the hut was about to come crashing down.

When things could not possibly get any worse, Flurry heard a voice from behind them. "You two! Get to your feet! What are you doing here?" Flurry turned and saw the arctic fox that had been commanding the fire beasts. "I'm General Nero of the Majesty's royal army! You shall answer when I speak to you!"

Flurry was frightened and slowly inched his way behind Lotora's legs. He even used her tail to hide beneath.

Nero looked right at Flurry. "You there! Little one! I haven't seen you before. Who are you, and what are you doing here?"

Flurry did not answer. His chin quivered as he tried to fight back tears. The white fox frightened him, and Flurry badly wanted to go back home, where it was safe.

"I'll give you to the count of three. One, two, ..."

Before the fox reached the number three, a loud voice from within the burning hut shouted, "Run!"

Suddenly, swords cut through the wall, and two red pandas burst out from the walls of the burning hut. The villagers scattered. Flurry and Lotora ran for their lives.

The male red panda was arrayed in red samurai armor, and the female wore silky robes singed by the flames. Both of them were armed with bladed weapons. Flurry glanced back and observed Tomodachi let out a war cry. He and the female red panda attacked Nero and fought in a two-on-one swordfight. Nero appeared to be holding his own against his two smaller opponents.

The raccoon villagers continued to run for their lives; the sound of metal on metal rang through the village. Flurry kept looking back to find Honja, but the hut collapsed, and not a single sign of the rabbit could be seen. Flurry cried and fell to the ground in tears. Lotora ran back and picked him up. "We can't fall behind. We need to keep going. We'll meet up with Tomodachi and ask him about Honja at the rendezvous point."

Flurry did not care about her attempt to comfort him. Now being carried away, he cried and shouted over Lotora's shoulder, "Honja! Honja!"

CHAPTER 3
THE HILLS

That night was one of the roughest Flurry had ever experienced. He was unable to rest. His eyes ached from his lamenting. Nothing Lotora said or did helped cheer him up.

The sun broke the horizon, and most of the raccoons met up under a large tree on a hill that overlooked a valley. This was their designated meeting place if anything were to happen to the village. From time-to-time, a few stragglers would show up. Not everyone was accounted for, but a majority of the village made it out safely.

Flurry sat on a log and stared at the ground. Nothing broke his gaze until the sound of loud bird-like whistle was heard. It was their lookout in the tree. Someone or something approached their position.

Two red pandas drew near, a male and a female. The male was middle-aged and the female was in her late teens.

Everyone stood up and bowed to the two figures when they entered the camp. Flurry looked up and realized that it was Tomodachi and Yujin. Flurry could not contain himself – he got up and ran to Tomodachi. The bear cub did not know that his behavior was not acceptable in red panda culture. Tomodachi was highly respected and revered. No one dared rush up to him like Flurry did. Such an act was considered to be disrespectful, rude, or worse. In some cases, samurai like Tomodachi have mistaken quick advances, like Flurry's, as an attack.

"Honja! Is he okay? Where's Honja?" Flurry shouted at the samurai.

Tomodachi looked straight at Flurry. It was difficult for anyone to tell what he was thinking. He had a stern facial expression. The samurai grunted. He turned toward Yujin, nodded his head at her, and walked off.

"Hey!" Flurry called out to Tomodachi. "I'm talking to you!"

Tomodachi paused, turned back, and shouted, "Kawaii! Look!"

Flurry looked and saw Yujin get down on one knee. Tears filled his eyes. Flurry certain that she was about to break the bad news to him. She reached for her pouch and lifted the flap. Flurry did not want to look. To see his lifeless friend would be too much to bear. Yujin held her pouch open and out popped a brown, furry head with two elongated ears.

Flurry could not believe his eyes. "Honja!" Flurry was so excited that he cried tears of joy.

"*Annyeong*," the rabbit replied and waved to his friend.

Flurry grabbed Honja, pulled him up from the bag, and gave him a hug. Honja felt uncomfortable, but he understood why Flurry had been concerned. He, too, thought he would die in the fire during the previous night's chaos.

Yujin stood back up and addressed Lotora. "We would've died if not for that rabbit. Someone had strapped the hideout door shut. We don't know who, but we think someone in the camp did it. We may have a spy among us."

Some raccoons were within earshot. They gasped when they heard the terrible report. The villagers deliberated with each other. Concerned expressions dominated their faces.

Their voices gained in volume as their fear grew. Panic was sure to ensue and spread among them like wildfire. Tomodachi stepped up on a rock and called out, "*Ya me te!* Stop! Everything … okay." Tomodachi was not fluent in their language, but he spoke well enough that everyone understood him.

Flurry approached Lotora and pulled her aside. "If it's okay with you, Honja and I would like to go back home now. Would you send us back, please?"

The raccoon knelt down to Flurry's eye level. Lotora looked at the bear cub empathetically and replied, "Oh, Flurry, that isn't how it works. The book doesn't send you where you want to go; it takes you where you need to be."

"No! That can't be true! I need to go home. Let me see that book!" Flurry ripped the book away from her arms, unlatched it, and turned pages. He touched the pictures with his paw, but nothing happened. Flurry dropped to the ground and sobbed. "How do we get home?"

Lotora's gaze fell. She felt sorry for the little cub and his rabbit companion. Just then, Tomodachi approached and ordered, "*Kawaii!* Up!"

"Huh?" Flurry replied.

"He's telling you to stand up," Lotora translated.

Flurry stood at attention and saluted Tomodachi. "Yes, sir!"

Honja hid behind Flurry. Tomodachi was an immensely intimidating presence. "Where … from?" Tomodachi asked.

Before Flurry could answer, Lotora stepped in and bowed to Tomodachi. "May I?" she asked. The samurai nodded his head. The raccoon spoke in a different language; Yujin acted as the translator. Tomodachi stroked the fur of his chin as he stood and listened. He nodded his head and then turned his attention to Flurry.

"This … true?"

Flurry had no idea what Tomodachi meant. "Is what true?" he asked. Yujin repeated Flurry's words in a language that Tomodachi understood.

"Jack … dead?" replied the samurai.

"Yes, but that hasn't happened yet, according to raccoon lady here," Flurry pointed at Lotora.

"How?" the samurai asked.

Flurry explained what had happened and then told him the story he heard from Vallidore on his last adventure. Tomodachi seemed particularly interested in that bit of information. A hint of a smile came to his face before he huffed, turned, and walked away.

"What did I say?" Flurry asked.

Lotora answered for him. "You didn't say anything wrong. He's in a good mood. At least, I think he is."

"He doesn't look like he's in a good

mood," replied the bear cub.

"Yes, well, he's a hard one to read, but you'll get used to it."

"Why does he call me ka … k … Kawaii? What does that mean?"

"It means 'cute'," Lotora replied.

"Oh! In that case, he can keep calling me that," Flurry answered. Honja shook his head in disbelief. Flurry obviously still had his issues with vanity. Honja half expected Flurry to demand everyone else to call him that from now on.

Tomodachi stood at a distance and spoke with the village leaders before he returned to speak with Yujin and Lotora. When he walked away, Lotora rushed over to Flurry. "Get up! We're moving out," she said.

"Where?" Flurry asked.

"Tomodachi is going to escort the

raccoons to a safe haven, and then we're going to meet up with samurai that are loyal to Tomodachi. He hopes to enlist their help. You've inspired him … I think."

Honja tapped his paw on Flurry's leg. Flurry turned to find Honja shaking like a leaf. The little rabbit wagged his head in fear. "Awww! There, there. Everything will be okay," Flurry tried to assure his friend. The bear cub bent down and patted Honja on the head.

Honja was instantly outraged and grunted at Flurry for having touched him. "Oops! Sorry, Honja. I keep forgetting." Honja replied with a sigh followed by muttering in a language that Flurry did not understand.

Flurry was so busy talking to Honja that he did not notice the raccoons had already started down the hill to the valley below. A loud shout broke. *"Kawaii!* Come!" Tomodachi commanded.

Startled by Tomodachi's authoritative demeanor, Flurry jumped up, scooped Honja up in his arms, and ran after the caravan of raccoons.

Traveling was the hardest part about all of Flurry's adventures. The land was so vast that it seemed to take forever to get anywhere. Simply going down into the valley and crossing an expansive meadow felt like it took the entire day. In the past, Flurry had something faster to ride on, like a wolf. Going on foot was excruciatingly slow, and the cub hated every bit of it.

A day and a half had now passed, and they were at a stretch of hills. The grass was orange instead of green, and Flurry was pleased that the company came to a stop so they could all rest. Flurry drank some water from a canteen Tomodachi had given him at the beginning of their trek.

Tomodachi, Yujin, and Lotora spoke with one another. Periodically, the three of them would look over at Flurry during their conversation. Flurry perceived that he was being talked about. Lotora finally nodded in agreement with the red pandas, broke away, and came toward Flurry and Honja.

"You two are coming with Yujin and me. We're going to meet back up with Tomodachi later," Lotora instructed.

"Why? What's going on?" Flurry asked.

"We're being tracked. Nero and his troops aren't far behind us. Tomodachi caught sight of a scout no more than an hour ago."

Flurry agreed to go with the ladies. Yujin let Honja get back into her pouch, and

Lotora put Flurry in her backpack where she kept her book. The raccoon's pack was very roomy, and Flurry could move around freely. Lotora and Yujin ran for a grouping of hills as Tomodachi gave instructions to the other raccoons.

Flurry and company were already at the hills when loud howls were heard. They looked back toward the group and saw three flaming fox creatures coming toward Tomodachi and the raccoon villagers. Flurry could not believe his eyes when he saw the event that unfolded. Tomodachi was a magnificent swordsman. Flurry's jaw dropped open as he watched the masterful samurai cut down all three of the beasts. The raccoons, meanwhile, ran for their lives. Flurry had a greater sense of security now that he knew what Tomodachi was capable of. Flurry reflected on his last adventure with Chingu and thought that he and Tomodachi were alike in many ways, except that Chingu was nicer.

Nightfall came. Lotora and Yujin set up camp in the hills. It had now been a full two days since they began their travels. Flurry felt weary. "Are we there yet?" he whined.

"No, but we should arrive by noon tomorrow," answered Yujin. She sat and sharpened one of her blades.

Flurry was a bit surprised. Yujin had not spoken much in a language he could understand. In fact, Flurry did not know she could speak his language so well, but all doubts about that had now been put to rest.

Being the curious cub he was, Flurry asked, "So why does it take both of you to speak to Tomodachi?"

Lotora chuckled and glanced over at the red panda. Yujin looked back and nodded with approval. It was her way of giving Lotora permission to tell Flurry what he wanted to know. "Well, Yujin and I speak the same language, but Tomodachi is from a different culture than Yujin. He knows our language too, but not fluently. Luckily, she can speak many different languages. So she can translate more clearly for Tomodachi."

"Oh … but I thought all red pandas came from the same place," Flurry replied.

"Yes and no. Yes, they all come from the land of Nallan Min. No, they don't all share the same culture and language. There are many different clans, but three of these clans are the most prominent. Many of them have been at war with each other for generations. However, two clans found a way to bring peace. It's mandatory in the culture of these two clans that each year a selected group of male members of one clan are given a wife from the female members of the other clan. That was their way to resolve generations of enmity. This new rule ensures that they'll always be united. They have a big official holiday celebration every year.

"Now, the other clans, that's another matter. Not all of them have made peace with each other."

"I thought you said that Jack is killing off the red pandas?" Flurry inquired.

"Yes, he is," answered Lotora.

"Then, why don't they all get together against Jack, instead of fighting each other? Aren't they doing Jack's work for him?"

Flurry's words impacted Yujin. She looked up and smiled. You could almost see a glimmer in her eyes. She turned to Lotora and spoke something in her native language. The female warrior then got up, walked over to her blanket, and laid down to sleep.

"What? What did she say?" Flurry insisted.

Lotora smiled and said, "She said that you remind her of her father. She's quite fond of you and hopes that you'll always keep this hope and bravery alive within you. It's souls like yours that change the world for the better."

Flurry did not know what to say, but he felt good about Yujin's words. Flurry yawned and was followed by Lotora doing likewise. They all agreed to call it a night. Each of them picked a spot around the camp fire and nestled up under their blankets.

Honja and Lotora were fast asleep, but

Flurry stayed awake for a bit. He thought about the past couple of days. He was beginning to feel more at ease and now remembered what it was that he loved about his adventures. Maybe tomorrow he could save the world with Tomodachi and stop Jack all over again.

Before long, Flurry found himself dozing off. No more sounds were heard but the crickets chirping and the fire crackling as the four slept through the night.

CHAPTER 4
RONIN

The next morning was off to a great start. The ladies packed up the camp and then headed out with the little ones in tow. As predicted, they arrived at their destination by noon. This particular day was hotter and more humid than the previous, so Flurry felt dreadful being in the noonday sun. However, they approached a town, which sparked Flurry's interest because it meant he would have shade, food, and something to drink.

They arrived at the old town known as Cliffside Peak. This place was unlike any that Flurry had ever seen before. A massive rock cliff draped the entire town in its shadow. The buildings were stone with ceramic roofs. The canopies, curtains, shutters, and other decorations were all red against a very lush, green backdrop. The color of red contrasted the green splendidly and made for a unique-looking town.

The town had a variety of different animals, from raccoons, to mice, rats, and even chipmunks, which Flurry thought were so adorable – but not as adorable as he was. The town was a haven for pirates, bounty hunters, mercenaries, and other shady characters with even shadier occupations.

All eyes were on them as they walked the streets. Unbeknownst to Flurry, Honja, or even Lotora, Tomodachi had already arrived. He had left secret clues on where to find him. Only Yujin knew how to decipher his code. She and her father devised a secret method of communication long ago. The clues were strewn about by a ribbon here or a marking there.

Before long, they came to an inn. "This will do," Yujin informed the others.

They entered and were met by the innkeeper. "We're all out of rooms," the keeper informed them. Flurry looked around. The establishment appeared to be empty.

"Surely you're not." Yujin softly answered.

"Well, that doesn't matter. Even if I had any rooms, I'm not going to house a red panda. Jack Frost could have my head for something like tha …"

Before the opossum could finish his sentence, he found a blade at his neck. "I could have your head, too." Yujin asked once more, "Are you absolutely sure there aren't any vacancies?"

The opossum stumbled around to find his words. The innkeeper finally answered. "Oh, well what do you know? There is a room. I must have overlooked it."

Yujin put away her sword and handed the innkeeper a gold coin. His eyes bulged at the sight of it. "Where did you get this?" he asked with astonishment. He looked at Yujin with tremendous interest in her answer.

"That's none of your business. Is it enough?" Yujin asked.

"Enough? This is a very rare coin. It's enough to buy the entire inn!" answered the opossum.

"Good! I can trust you to keep your mouth shut, then?"

"Of course! You were never here. I saw nothing. Here's your key. Go up the steps, turn left, and it's the last room on the right."

Yujin took the key and led her companions to the room. After entering, she locked the door and rushed over to the window to draw the curtains. "We won't be safe here for very long. We'll head out very soon. We're only here to meet my father and figure out our next plan."

"How will he know where to find us?" Flurry asked as he climbed out of Lotora's backpack.

"He already has," answered Lotora. She motioned with her head.

Flurry looked up and saw Tomodachi

standing in the room. "How did you …?"

Flurry's sentence was cut off. "*Kawaii!* No talk!" Tomodachi turned to his daughter and spoke with her. While they deliberated, Tomodachi's ears perked up. He raised his paw, and the other two were instantly silent. A creaking sound came from outside the room. Tomodachi and Yujin immediately withdrew their swords.

"*Kawaii!* Hide!" Tomodachi ordered in a whisper.

Flurry grabbed Honja and clambered inside the wardrobe. They both sat quietly in the dark and peeked through the crack between the closed doors. The creaking sound was heard again. It appeared to either be from steps in the hall or on the roof.

Flurry did not have to wonder for very long. The door to the room burst open, and a variety of rodent opportunists barged in. "We're here to take you in. There's quite a bounty on your heads, dead or alive," spoke the leader of the scraggly-looking band of creeps. He was a rat, both in appearance and actions. The rodent had his sword drawn and pointed at the samurai's face.

Tomodachi huffed with amusement. "You sure 'bout dis?" questioned the samurai.

"Certainly!" replied the rat.

At that moment, a swooshing sound was heard. Whatever happened, it was so fast that Flurry did not see it. The rat fell to the floor, dead.

"Next?" asked Tomodachi.

The other rodents cowered in fear. They each backed out of the entryway slowly before they turned and ran away.

"We're in trouble! If they were going to

turn us in, then Nero must already be here!" Lotora made her concerns known.

Yujin agreed, and walked out of the room with her father. They looked down from the banister and caught site of none other than Nero himself. The one-armed arctic fox stood at the entrance of the inn and questioned the rodents. The innkeeper looked up at Tomodachi and made a motion with his head to inform them to get out while they still could. Tomodachi peered down from the balcony at his enemy. One of the rodents pointed up toward the room. Nero turned. His gaze was met by his rival. An angry scowl came to each of their faces.

"That one, right there! He's mine! Kill the rest!" Nero ordered his troops. He had a lot of backup this time. There were dozens of arctic foxes armed to the teeth with weaponry.

Tomodachi had a smirk on his face when he addressed Nero. "Missing some-ting?" Nero shook with rage. Their last battle in Coonlei cost him dearly. It was apparent Tomodachi was responsible for Nero's missing arm.

The arctic foxes ran up the steps toward Tomodachi, but were met with Yujin's blade. A heated battle broke out. The clanging and clashing of metal resounded throughout the inn. The innkeeper looked on in horror. He helplessly watched as his establishment got ripped apart. He clutched his gold coin tightly and hastily ran out of the inn.

"Archers!" shouted Nero. Within seconds, a division of white foxes came in with flaming arrows. "Light this place up!" Nero commanded.

Without hesitation, flames shot through the air at Tomodachi and Yujin. "Fall back!" Tomodachi ordered his daughter.

They both retreated into their room and pushed the wardrobe in front of the door. "We need to get out of here!" shouted Lotora.

"Indeed!" answered Tomodachi while he spread the curtains and opened the window. Tomodachi whistled loudly, and then turned to the others. "Come! Roof escape!"

They all climbed out of the window and onto the roof. Nero's soldiers littered the streets. "Come!" Tomodachi shouted. He raced across the roof and leapt to the next building. Their fox rivals pursued from street level. Flaming arrows rained across the sky. The town was quickly engulfed in fire. From rooftop to rooftop they glided, with Flurry and Honja in tow.

Shouting and chaos broke out in the streets. Many of the town's inhabitants were angry about their home being set ablaze, so they took out their aggression on Nero's troops, which resulted in a full-blown riot.

Tomodachi took advantage of the much-needed distraction and leapt to the vine-covered rock cliff near the edge of the town's roofline. Yujin and the others followed. They climbed the vines, desperately trying to reach the top of the cliff.

The climb was arduous and terrifying. Flurry wondered what was in store for them next. They did not have horses to outrun Nero's army. However, Tomodachi seemed unconcerned about their predicament.

Tomodachi whistled again. A flying creature swooped down low enough for the red panda and the others to jump onto its back. The winged beast caught them and soared over the burning town below.

Nero watched on in anger. He muttered to himself, "You can run, but I'll catch you!"

The creature glided through the air so majestically. Flurry could not believe what had happened. Adrenaline rushed over him. "Yay!" Flurry shouted. Honja, on the other hand, hid in Yujin's pouch. The rabbit made certain to keep his eyes covered at all times. He was not fond of the flight at all.

The beast had one set of wings to glide upon, four legs, and a tail. Its body was covered with a dense set of crimson-colored scales. The creature's head had various horns that protruded outward. It reminded

Flurry of a dragon, but smaller than what he expected.

Being the curious fellow he was, Flurry inquired, "Mr. Red Panda?" Flurry called out again and tugged on Tomodachi's arm. "Where did this dragon come from, and where are we going?"

Tomodachi smirked and replied, "My pet. Go north."

Lotora interjected. "This creature is a reeyu. They're the most intelligent of all creatures. As infants, they can communicate with any of the animals. This helps them to survive during their early years. It's unknown how they acquired this ability, though."

"How old is this one?" Flurry asked.

"This is an adolescent reeyu. Only the greatest of the red panda warriors can ride an adolescent reeyu. Most of the red pandas commandeer infant reeyu, because they're easier to control. Adolescent reeyu can be extremely fierce and difficult to break," Lotora expounded.

Flurry could not contain his excitement. "Honja! We're riding a dragon!" Flurry shouted. When he did not receive a reply, he looked into Yujin's pouch and said, "Honja?"

Honja still cowered inside. He was not about to acknowledge Flurry in any way, at least not until his paws were on solid ground again.

Flurry gazed out in awe. He could see so far across the landscape below. It was like he could see everything at once. He had no idea how fast the reeyu was gliding, but they were making excellent time. The town they had left burning was now so far in the distance that not even the smoke could be seen any longer.

The reeyu swooped lower to the ground and glided in through a massive canyon. The river below roared loudly. The water wildly twisted to and fro through the canyon.

They progressed farther up the canyon. Flurry viewed a spectacle unlike anything he had seen before. A massive city was hidden in plain sight. It had been built into the walls of the canyon, and was beautiful beyond words. Other reeyu flew around, and Flurry could see that the city was populated by other red panda warriors dressed similarly to Tomodachi.

The city was carved back into the rock face, and platforms had been built to extend out from the canyon walls for the reeyu to land on. Everything was intricately decorated, and the dark hue of green starkly contrasted the pale stone.

Their winged ride swooped down to a platform and landed gracefully. After it touched down, the reeyu knelt to allow its passengers to disembark.

Flurry climbed down, ran over to the edge, and looked down at the raging water below. A shadow engulfed the bear. He looked up and beheld another reeyu as it flew overhead. "Oooh!" Flurry exclaimed.

Honja was free from Yujin's pouch. Flurry motioned him over. "Honja, come quickly! You have to see this!"

Honja shook his head and trailed behind Lotora. Flurry decided to join the party and skipped up to them.

"*Kawaii!* Come!" Tomodachi hollered to

the bear cub. Flurry rushed up to him. The samurai pointed at an enclosure filled with infant reeyu. "For you!"

Flurry was shocked by his statement. He looked up and said, "One of them is for me?" Tomodachi nodded. "Yay!" Flurry climbed over the fence and patted the baby reeyu on their heads. Each reeyu looked different. They ranged in shape, size, and color. "I wonder which one I should choose."

Yujin walked up and interrupted him. "It doesn't work like that. Your reeyu will choose you."

Flurry was giddy as could be. All of the reeyu were so adorable. Then one of them took a particular interest in him. This reeyu had a purple tone to its scales, and its wings were very small, barely big enough to do anything. It was unlikely that this reeyu could fly. It came up to Flurry, sniffed him, and rubbed up against him as if it were a cat.

"Looks like you found your reeyu," Yujin informed the bear. "She likes you."

"She? You mean it's a … a girl?" Flurry's countenance wavered. "I don't want a girl dragon!" Flurry exclaimed. At that moment, the reeyu licked him on the cheek. "Ewww! She licked me! Ick! Yuck! Dragon germs!" Flurry wiped his fur frantically.

The little reeyu let out a miniature roar and pounced on the cub. Flurry was knocked onto his back, and the reeyu continued to vigorously lick his face. Everyone laughed. Even Honja pointed and giggled – which was a nice change for him.

Tomodachi gave a slight hint of a smile, bowed to Flurry, and walked off. "We'll have to saddle her up for you before we leave," said Yujin.

Flurry came out of the enclosure and tried to brush himself clean. "Leave? Can't we stay for a while?" Flurry insisted.

Lotora answered him. "Yes, we'll stay here for a while, so we may rest and figure out what we should do next."

"I know what we should do. We should put an end to Jack. I did it before, and I can do it again," Flurry confidently bellowed.

Some of the other red pandas heard him, and they whispered amongst each other. One of them came up to Yujin and spoke in a concerned tone. "What's this I hear? Are you mad? Nobody can take on Jack! It would be suicide!"

The red panda would have continued, but Tomodachi returned and interrupted him.

"Yes! Much glory! Honorable death!"

"There aren't enough of you to take on his entire army. He has at least a legion of polar bears with him in Ursidea, not to mention the army at Ursadoom. Nero commands Jack's arctic fox division. There are entire nations loyal to him," retorted one of the red pandas from the crowd which now stood around them.

"Those nations are only loyal out of fear. They aren't true allies. If enough of the kingdoms turn on Jack, the others will join in the rebellion, too," Yujin replied.

Another red panda chimed in. "This is madness! This can never be done! Even with an army! You forget that he has command over the ice and snow. He can turn any of us into a pillar of ice whenever he wishes to do so."

Many red pandas had now closed in on the debate and became involved in the grumbling.

"Silence! We shall fight Jack, with or without your help!" Yujin bellowed.

Tomodachi stood up, shouted, "Decision, made!" and that was the end of it. The conversation came to a close when Tomodachi stormed off.

The evening came, and it was a very peaceful one at that. They were out of harm's way for the time being. Residing down in the canyon gave them shade, and the mist from a nearby waterfall felt great when the wind occasionally blew some of the water in their direction.

Flurry and the others were taken to a set of guest quarters; they were the nicest and most luxurious rooms Flurry had ever seen.

The best part of all was the array of delicious food. Flurry could eat his heart out and die happy. He was in paradise. Even Honja appeared to enjoy himself. He nibbled on a big carrot that sat in front of him. Flurry caught him cuddling with it a few times, though Honja denied it.

Lotora looked out the window and stared at the moon now risen over the canyon. Tomodachi stood outside the room with Yujin and discussed their plans. Lotora took note of their conversation and then entered the room to rejoin Flurry and Honja.

"So what's the name of this place? I want to come here again someday," Flurry asked.

"Does it even exist in your time?" Lotora puzzled.

"Good question. I have no idea," Flurry replied.

"This city is named Ronin. It's the last safe haven for the red pandas. Most of the warriors here are on their own. Many of their masters died in battle, fighting Jack. All of us have suffered losses from Jack." Lotora's eyes filled with tears.

"What's wrong? Are you okay?" Flurry asked. He ran over and gave her a hug.

"Yes. I'm just recalling the memory of my husband and daughter."

"Are they okay?"

"No, they're not. Jack killed my husband, and I don't wish to speak of my daughter's fate. Now you see why we all live in fear, and why we need the hope of seeing an end come to Jack's reign of terror. Your presence is the sign that we've all needed for so long," Lotora explained and hugged Flurry in return.

At this time, Yujin and Tomodachi entered the room. Yujin sat down across from Lotora and Flurry. She looked right at the bear cub and said, "Tell me how my father defeats Jack."

"I have no idea. I just know that he does. Doggy told me so," Flurry answered.

"And you're sure of this?"

"Uh huh!" Flurry nodded his head. He was very sure of himself.

"First, we're going to need all of the allies we can get. My father has already made a pact with the warriors here in Ronin. Tomorrow we shall head out to neighboring nations to ask for their help."

"You should ask for Santa to help, too!" Flurry interjected.

"Santa?" Yujin replied. She was perplexed.

"I think he means Nikolas Kringle," Lotora added.

"Nobody has seen him in years. I'd have no idea where to look," Yujin answered.

"Has anyone tried Ursus?" Flurry asked.

"Ursus?" the red panda was still uncertain what Flurry meant.

"He means the land of Mezarim," Lotora responded.

"Why would anyone want to live up there?" Yujin inquired.

"Exactly!" Flurry replied. "That makes it the perfect hideout!"

Tomodachi sat and listened. He looked at his daughter and spoke to her before she turned back to address Flurry.

"Okay, my father says that he'll focus on gathering forces, while the rest of us search for Niko … I mean Santa. If we can find him, he'll be a tremendous aid to our cause. I only hope he's still on good terms with the elves. Not many think well of that man," Yujin mentioned.

"Very well, then. Let's get some shut-eye. Tomorrow will be a big day," Lotora replied, ending the discussion.

The four agreed and called it a night. They would need their rest. Little did any of them know what was in store for them on the morrow.

CHAPTER 5
EBONGREENE FOREST

BOOM! The walls shook, and trumpets blared. Flurry flew out of bed. He was on his feet at such speed that you would have thought he had wings. It was a rude awakening from a peaceful night of sleep. BOOM! The tremendous sound of impacts echoed throughout the canyon. Flurry peeked out the window and saw red pandas scurrying in every direction.

The chaos intensified with the deafening noise of collapsing stone. Walls crumbled into the water below. The thundering explosions resonated throughout the entire city.

"What's going on?" Flurry called out from the window.

"We're under attack!" shouted a red panda that rushed past, sword drawn.

Flurry heard samurai in the distance shout, "Take cover! Another salvo is incoming!" BOOM! The floor rumbled and shook beneath the cub's feet. In terror, Flurry watched one of the city walls collapse.

Flurry glanced around the room. Honja hid under a pillow, but no one else was present. "Come on, Honja! We have to get out of here!" Honja refused. Flurry ran over and dragged the bunny away from the pillow. "We're leaving, even if I have to carry you!"

Flurry ran out through the open archway with Honja in his arms. Rocks fell all around him, and walls buckled. Many of the platforms and bridges were no longer intact.

Flurry tried to speak over all of the noise. "I have no idea how we're going to get out of this mess, Honja." The cub frantically looked around for an answer when he heard reeyu hatchlings screeching and crying. Flurry ran to the gate of the enclosure and loosed them. "Go! You're free! Go!" The reeyu infants ran out as fast as they could. Flurry looked around to find many of the reeyu adults dead. Tears formed in Flurry's eyes, but he took in a deep breath and wiped them away. It was not the time or place to grieve; that would have to wait for later. Flurry knew he had to be brave. He looked up and noticed that the reeyu traveled along the same path together. The cub followed the reeyu babies close behind. He thought they must know of a way out he was unaware of.

Before Flurry got far, he heard another reeyu screech from behind him. He turned around and found his own reeyu. She stood by, already saddled. Flurry was pleased to see her. "Come here, girl!" he motioned for her to join him. The reeyu ran to him. Flurry got on her back with Honja still in his arms. Together, they rode after the other reeyu. The canyon walls collapsed all around them. Boulders crashed in their path, which forced numerous course corrections.

Flurry had no idea what was happening, nor did he know where Tomodachi, Yujin, or Lotora were. He felt a tremendous amount of fear and uncertainty in the midst of such chaos. Red panda warriors continued to frantically run in every direction.

The baby reeyu found a cliff-side path that went along the canyon wall. Flurry followed it, and hoped that it led to the surface above. Flurry's reeyu ran as hard as her little legs would take her. In her haste, Honja slipped out of Flurry's arms and slid down her tail. The rabbit hung on for dear life.

They were almost out of the chaos when the unthinkable happened. A flaming boulder flew across the sky and struck the stone path. BOOM! The side of the cliff gave way and collapsed into the rapids below. "Back up girl, back up! You can do it." Flurry patted her scaly hide, with the reins in one paw.

The little reeyu managed to get turned around and ran back toward one of the city's platforms. It appeared they would make it, until the remaining path gave way. "Ahhh!" Flurry screamed as he and his reeyu fell to the depths below.

Honja, on the other hand, landed on the platform right when the reeyu swung her tail, which caused him to lose his grip. Honja dashed to the edge of the platform, looked down, and saw Flurry and his reeyu crash into the rushing waters. Tears filled Honja's eyes as he scanned the river's surface for any sign of them, but there was none.

Honja felt lost and all alone. He had no idea what to do. The rabbit collapsed in tears, but soon heard a familiar voice from behind. "Honja!" called Yujin. She ran up to him and scooped him up in her arms. "Where's Flurry?" Honja pointed down toward the base of the canyon. "Oh no!" Yujin responded. She turned around and shouted to her father. "We need you! Flurry's in trouble!"

"No! We go!" Tomodachi ordered.

Lotora ran up behind Yujin. "I can't find Flurry or Honja anywhere," she said.

"Honja is here, but Flurry fell into the river. The danger is too great; we can't stay here. We'll have to send out a search party later, assuming we can escape. Nero has Ronin surrounded," Yujin replied.

Lotora gasped at the news. She ran to the edge, and looked down at the raging rapids. While Yujin spoke, Lotora stood there and thought about Flurry. She knew that nobody could survive that kind of a fall, nor avoid drowning in a river that fierce. Lotora's chin quivered and tears came to her eyes. She knew Flurry was dead.

"Lotora! Come on!" shouted Yujin.

Lotora snapped out of her trance. She turned to follow Yujin and Tomodachi. The trio climbed the rock face together. The only way out was up, now that most of the reeyu had fled or died in the attack. When they reached the surface, they were met by dozens of arctic foxes with swords and bows drawn.

Nero approached. "Put down your weapons; you've been defeated," commanded the white fox.

Tomodachi refused to do such a thing. To give up would be dishonorable. It was more honorable for him to die in battle. He reached for his sword, but the soldiers swept in and took his weapons before they bound him and the others.

"Look at you now! Not so tough are you?" Nero remarked cruelly. He punched Tomodachi in the face. "I would love to make you suffer for taking my arm, but I have orders from Jack to bring you in …" His voice trailed off, then after a sigh of regret he concluded his sentence. "… Unharmed."

He looked Yujin over and then brought his gaze back to Tomodachi before he continued. "You're lucky my master wants to make an example out of you, or else you would suffer my wrath. Making a spectacle of your failure should crush your foolish little rebellion."

With an evil smirk upon his face, Nero took a few steps away. He momentarily paused, turned back, and kicked Tomodachi in the face. In an angrier tone than before, Nero yelled, "And that's for my arm!"

"Sir! Our orders are to …" one of the foxes began. Nero shot an angry glance back toward his guard and barked orders. "I know! Take them away!" The other arctic foxes tied Yujin, Tomodachi, and Lotora's ropes to the back of a cart. The warriors all gathered together and formed a caravan. The carts, horses, and troops moved west. Their prisoners were led by their bindings. If any of them were to fall, they would be dragged through the dirt.

As the captives were strung along, Nero grinned at his evil thoughts and made parting remarks. "Enjoy your travels; we have a long way to go before we reach Ursidea. No worries though, Jack's making a special trip to meet us along the way. When we reach Ursidea, I'll enjoy watching you die the death you deserve, traitor! So you have until then to make your peace with whatever deity you believe in." The arctic fox laughed maniacally and walked off.

Nero saddled up and rode his horse out ahead of his company of warriors. Luckily for Honja, nobody realized he was there. The soldiers had removed all of the hostages' belts, pouches, bags, and weapons and placed them in the carriage. They did not think to search any of it, so Honja hid in silence.

While concealed, Honja debated what he should do. He was filled with regret over not being kinder to Flurry when he was still alive. The rabbit teared up at his thoughts of the horrors he had gone through, and he longed to be home with his mother. He prayed that this was merely a bad dream, and that it would all end soon.

The caravan was now well on its way to Ursidea and had traveled many miles, but they were being watched. From a nearby cliff, red panda warriors from Ronin stood ready. "We can't allow Tomodachi to be put to death. That will kill any hope we have of truly defeating Jack," the lead red panda stated to the others that stood near.

Another of the warriors replied to him. "We should continue to gather our forces on his behalf and round up as many as we can before they reach Ursidea. I surmise that we have at least a week or longer before they arrive."

All of the red pandas present nodded in agreement, mounted their reeyu, and took flight. They each split off in different directions.

Back at the canyon, nothing remained of Ronin but ruins. Down below, the river churned and rushed by wildly. The foamy waves crashed against the rocks and sucked down anything that plunged into its grip.

With waves bubbling violently, the water spun and turned as the torrent raced along its winding path. A scaly snout broke the surface of the water and gasped for breath. The baby reeyu was tossed to and fro as she fought to keep her head above the waves. The reeyu struggled to catch a glimpse of her bear cub master, but Flurry was nowhere to be found.

The reeyu gasped for air, but she kept getting pulled under the waves. The current was so strong that she could barely muster enough strength to come up. Every time she sank below the seething surface, she found herself tumbling fiercely in the undertow. She did not know if she could make it much longer. She made one final attempt to get her head above the chaos before her strength was depleted. This time she spotted a large branch close by. The reeyu quickly latched on to the floating log for dear life.

She rode the driftwood for some time before it wedged itself among some rocks. The reeyu climbed up from the log and onto the stones that protruded from the water at the riverbank's edge. She leapt from one to the next until she was safe on the shore. Once upon solid ground, she collapsed from and passed out from exhaustion.

When the little reeyu opened her eyes again, night had fallen. The stars twinkled brightly, and the moon gleamed from above. She felt a bit stronger. The reeyu decided that she needed to figure out what to do next. She saw something on the river bank, only a short jog down from her position. It looked like another animal.

She rushed down to investigate, and what she discovered was disheartening. It was Flurry, but he was nearly dead. He was not moving, and his breathing was very shallow. She came up and nudged him with her nose, but Flurry did not respond. She pushed him again; he showed no sign of acknowledgment. The reeyu licked him, since that always elicited a reaction from the young cub. Unfortunately, it was also met with silence.

The reeyu cried and let out a loud screech. Her tears flowed down her face. She cuddled up next to Flurry and cradled him, but he did not reciprocate anything more than a faint groan.

Flurry's reeyu knew she had to do something, or else Flurry would die. She did not know what to do; she was only an infant. She really needed some help.

The reeyu stood up, opened her mouth, and made strange sounds that were impossible to describe – only one who has observed a reeyu could understand.

She vigilantly called out and screeched at the night sky, as if she were a wolf howling at the moon. This went on for an immeasurable amount of time, but then something happened.

Out from the brush came many animals of every shape, size, and kind. There were rabbits, mice, deer, birds, bears, beavers, groundhogs, squirrels, and many more. The infant reeyu all had a special ability to communicate with the animals, and she called upon them for help.

The beavers chewed down some trees while the deer helped to remove the branches. Bears came and moved the trees to make a bridge across the river. The birds flew off and returned with vines. Some coyotes drew near. The lifted Flurry up and set him, face down, on the reeyu infant's back, while the birds used the vines to tie him in place so that he would not fall off. The squirrels brought some of their stash of nuts to provide food for the reeyu on her journey.

The reeyu asked the animals where to take Flurry. They informed her, all in their own manner of communication, that she needed to take him to a hermit up in the hills of Ebongreene Forest.

Determined to find this hermit, the little reeyu was now as prepared as she could be. She set off on her journey. Time was of the essence. She knew she had to find this reclusive individual if she were ever going to save Flurry's life, which was now waning.

Her journey seemed to take forever as she crossed hills, grasslands, and plains. She traveled through forests and through an infamous wasteland known as Crocodune. Every step of the way she grew weaker, but she pushed herself further. She knew she must save her teddy bear master.

Finally, she reached the edge of Ebongreene Forest, but she was too weak to venture in. The little reeyu collapsed to the ground and was about to pass out from exhaustion. Her vision blurred, and her eyelids became heavy. Before she lost consciousness, she saw several figures come toward her.

Out of the forest appeared half a dozen furry creatures. They appeared, to the reeyu, to be teddy bears. The bears ran up to her and gave her some water. As she came back around, a white bear, dressed in armor, approached her.

The little bear laid down his shield and knelt next to the reeyu. "Where did you come from?" he asked. As he pulled her up for a drink, he noticed she had a passenger. "There's a rider! Cut them free!" ordered the ivory-colored bear.

The other bears cut Flurry free and set him on the ground next to the reeyu. The reeyu looked at her fuzzy friend with deep grief in her eyes. She groaned and cried for her master. "Shhhhh! Hush now, your friend will be fine," came the voice of a female bear with yellow fur. She patted the reeyu to reassure her.

The bear knight looked closely at the cub and was startled. "Flurry? What's he doing here?" the bear asked himself. He stood up and shouted, "Someone! Quick! Get Nick! It's an emergency!" The bear picked Flurry up in his arms, ran into the forest, and called out, "Nick! Nick! Come quickly! We need you! Nick!"

A young, muscular man rushed out from the wilderness to meet the bear. He was very tall, with dark brown hair that went down to the middle of his bare back. He sported a goatee with the ends braided and bore some sort of Celtic-looking knotwork on his right arm and chest.

The man met the white bear halfway and looked down at the nearly lifeless bear cub. As Flurry was placed on a patch of grass, the bear said to the gentleman, "Look! It's Flurry!"

The man was dumbfounded. He reached over, touched Flurry's arm, and then put his ear to the cub's mouth. "He's going to die," the man informed everyone that stood near. The other bears gasped, and the reeyu cried.

A young, red-haired lady with green eyes ran up and joined them. She had a bow in her right hand and a quiver of arrows at her side. "What's going on?" she asked.

"Katie, it's Flurry," the man answered her.

"How's this possible?" Katie replied.

"I don't know, but if I don't do something, he'll die."

At that moment, Flurry stopped breathing. Katie put one hand over her mouth and pointed with the other. "Oh, Nick! Do something!" Tears streamed down her cheeks.

"Would that be an abuse of the powers entrusted to me? Would I be breaking the rules?" Nick asked the beautiful lady.

"You need to do what's right, regardless of the rules," she insisted.

"You're right, of course." Nick leaned forward and whispered something in Flurry's ear. Suddenly, Flurry coughed up water and gasped for breath. Nick rolled Flurry to his side so he could spit the water out. "It's okay. Everything's okay now. Breathe. Just breathe."

Disoriented, Flurry looked up at the young man. It was evident that the cub was confused when he said, "San'ta?"

Katie and Nick glanced at each other with a perplexed expression upon each of their faces. Perhaps it was some form of baby speech? It strangely resembled the word for "father" in an ancient dialect of Mezarim. Nick cleared his throat and replied, "No, I'm not your father. My name is Nikolas."

Flurry replied, "Santa!" and clutched Nikolas around the neck with an affectionate hug. Amusement broke out among the teddy bears. They giggled, and Nikolas himself chuckled with them.

"Welcome back, Flurry," said the white bear in shiny armor.

"How do you know my name?" asked

Flurry.

"We've met before, don't you remember? It's me! Drift!" answered the bear.

Flurry looked at Drift's shield and noticed it bore a snowflake design that matched the one on Flurry's scarf. "Are you related to me?" Flurry inquired.

"No. It's just that I decided to choose this as my family crest like you advised me to do. Don't you remember?"

Flurry shook his head. He felt immensely confused. All the while, Nikolas was deep in thought. "Flurry, I'd like to ask you a question," Nikolas informed the cub.

"Okay?"

"How did you get here exactly? Was it by a book?"

"Yes! How did you know that?" Flurry felt that progress was finally being made.

"Pardon me for a moment." Nikolas grabbed Katie and stepped back apace. He asked Drift to join them. "I think he's from the future, and I think he hasn't yet visited us the first time. That's why he doesn't remember us, or what he told us about that special book of his. Remember what he said to you the first time he saw you, Drift?"

"Hmmm, that does make sense," answered Drift. "So if that's the case, what do we do now?"

"We need to find out why he's here and what has happened to him," Nikolas answered.

When their private chat was over, they turned and saw Flurry on his back. His reeyu was overjoyed at his return to the living. She had pounced him and licked his face repeatedly. "Okay, okay! I get it. You can stop now," Flurry insisted as he tried to push her off.

"Your reeyu truly loves you. She traveled all this way to save your life. We found her carrying you on her back, from wherever the two of you came," Drift informed the little cub.

"The last thing I remember was falling into a river," Flurry replied.

"What river? When?" asked Nikolas.

"We were in Running, and it got attacked by a mean white fox," answered Flurry.

Nikolas's eyes widened with astonishment. "Wait a minute! Do you mean Ronin?"

"Yeah, that's what I said! Running!"

"Nero attacked Ronin? Why would he do this? That's unprecedented!"

"He was probably trying to stop us,"

Flurry reasoned.

"Stop whom?"

"Me and my friends."

"And these friends might be …?"

"Tomodachi, Yujin, and Lotora. Oh, yeah, and my friend, Honja. I hope they're okay. I haven't seen them since the attack."

Nikolas glanced at Katie. They were both extremely bewildered. Nikolas continued. "You mean Tomodachi, the samurai?"

"Yeah! That's what I said. Why do you keep questioning me like that?" Flurry replied.

Nikolas reached over and picked up an object wrapped in cloth. He removed the fabric covering to reveal a beautiful sword.

"Hey! That's Chingu's sword!" Flurry shouted. "What are you doing with it?"

"The Great King gave this to me. He told

me to give it to Tomodachi. I had no idea where I would find him, and now here you are. So … where do I find him?" Nikolas asked.

"I don't know. He was trying to get others to join him in a fight against Jack," answered the cub.

Suddenly, everyone gasped and turned to their neighbor to whisper amongst themselves. One of the teddy bears asked, "So the prophecy is true?" The entire crowd was now abuzz.

Nikolas stood up and addressed them. "I don't know how Flurry ended up being a part of this, but it's obvious that he was chosen. This all has a purpose. He was sent so that we can put an end to Jack Frost's tyranny once and for all."

The bears cheered, but Drift was not so

quick to rejoice. "How are we going to do this without an army?" he asked. "Secondly, he doesn't even know where Tomodachi is!"

"But we do!" came another voice. Everyone turned and saw that three red panda warriors now stood among them. Their reeyu were perched on the rocks not far behind the trio.

Drift pulled his ax, and Katie drew her bow, but Nikolas raised his hands in the air. "Stay your weapons! All of you! They're welcome here!"

"Need I remind you that most of the nations want you dead?" Katie informed the young man.

"There'll be no bloodshed here! You're now my guests, and I bid you welcome," Nikolas insisted.

The red pandas came forward. The leader

quickly explained their presence. "We've been tracking that cub's reeyu, and it led us to you. The Great King is clearly with us all this day. Tomodachi has been taken captive and is being led to Ursidea as we speak. They should arrive within a week. Jack plans to make an example out of him."

"I see. Well, then, we haven't any time to waste. We need to gather as many allies as we can, and ride for Ursidea. This could be the answer we've longed for, after all of these years. Tomorrow, we leave at first light. To Ursidea!" Nikolas shouted.

"To Ursidea!" clamored the others.

Nightfall came again, and everyone had gathered up in the hills in Ebongreene Forest, where Nikolas took care of his guests.

They had a feast, sang, and were merry all

throughout the night. Flurry tried to enjoy himself, but he constantly worried about Honja and wondered if the little rabbit was okay.

Bedtime came for everyone, and Katie had made a comfy sleeping spot for Flurry. As she tucked him in, Nikolas entered the room. "Santa, why does my papa call you Chris, but everyone here calls you Nick?" Flurry asked.

Nikolas chuckled and said, "Christopher is my first name. I've never liked it much, so I go by my middle name, Nikolas."

"Santa is much better. You should go by that," Flurry replied. Nikolas and Katie laughed. "So how long have you been married?"

"Huh?" the two replied in unison. They were taken off guard by Flurry's question.

"Yeah, I mean, every time I go to your house, she makes me cookies. Do you have any cookies now? That would be wonderful! They're the best! Yum! Yum!" Flurry informed them.

"Uhhh … we aren't a couple. We're just friends," answered Katie.

"Oh. Well, maybe you need to think about that. You two are great together," Flurry answered and giggled.

Nikolas and Katie looked at each other and blushed.

"Well, it's time for you to get some shut-eye. We have a lot of work to do in the morning. Rest well and good night," said Nikolas as he and Katie walked out the door of Flurry's room. As they strolled out, Nikolas put his hand on the small of Katie's back. He spoke softly to her, and closed

Flurry's door.

Flurry smiled and said to himself, "Who's the matchmaker? I am!"

CHAPTER 6
LOTORA'S DEAL

While Flurry was safe in Ebongreene Forest, Tomodachi and his companions were extremely fatigued from their trek on foot. Lotora was so weak that she let the ropes drag her along in the dirt.

The troops took their three prisoners and put them on one of the wheeled carts to rest for a bit. Nero did not want Jack to be angry about the condition Tomodachi would arrive in. They were now all on the same cart with their belongings. Honja realized that this was his chance, if he could muster up enough courage to leave the pouch. He was very frightened. Honja closed his eyes, took in a deep breath, and peeked his head out. He saw Tomodachi, Yujin, and Lotora, weary and half asleep on the cart.

Honja slipped out of the bag. He snuck over to Yujin, and nibbled away at her bindings. It was going to take a while, but if anything was for certain, it was that they had plenty of time remaining on their trip.

After his diligent work, Honja was met with success and moved on to Tomodachi. Yujin remained asleep the entire time, but Tomodachi was aware of what was happening. Eyes still closed, a smirk came to Tomodachi's face. He knew that his chance to break free and seek revenge was at hand.

A few more nibbles, and Tomodachi was free from his ropes. Honja had succeeded. The red pandas had been liberated, and now it was time to loose Lotora.

Tomodachi nudged his daughter and slowly snuck up behind the drivers of the cart. A hint of a grin came to his face as he inched toward his sword. He could already taste victory. The blade lay on the bench between the two foxes at the helm of the cart. He turned his head back to Yujin, and she nodded.

The moments that followed were so sudden that the drivers of the carriage did not know what hit them. Tomodachi grabbed his sword and cut down his enemies like a hot knife through butter.

One of the horsemen looked back, saw the escaped prisoners, and sounded his horn.

Nero and the others spun around and glimpsed Tomodachi as he leapt from horse to horse. The samurai dispatched one fox after another.

"Somebody stop him!" Nero shouted.

Yujin had joined the battle, and chaos ensued. Lotora picked up Honja and attempted to hide. One-by-one, Nero's warriors were cut down like grass. Tomodachi was nearly unstoppable. He was a warrior of renown. It looked as if Tomodachi would defeat the entire company of soldiers singlehandedly, until Nero took matters into his own paws.

"Stop, if you want your friend to live!" shouted Nero.

Tomodachi turned and saw Lotora held captive.

"I have no idea how you three managed to

get free, but it ends now. I don't want to incur the wrath of my master. However, he'll have my head if I allow you to succeed," Nero continued.

"There's no need for concern," came another voice. "I'll deal with this personally." A legion of polar bears approached, led by Jack Frost. "Bring the prisoners to me!" Jack shouted.

Tomodachi and Yujin were disarmed and brought before Jack. He paced to and fro in front of them. Jack clapped his paws, and the red panda prisoners were shoved to their knees, along with Lotora. "That's better! It's only fitting that Tomodachi … the great Tomodachi … kneel before his ruler and master."

The samurai warrior said something in an unknown tongue, but it was undoubtedly a vulgarity of some kind. Jack smacked Tomodachi across the face. "Now, now! None of that kind of talk. We're gentlefolk, you and I, not barbarians. However, I may need to make an exception for the sake of teaching you a lesson." Jack looked at Nero and ordered, "His blade! Bring it to me!"

Nero came forth with Tomodachi's beautifully crafted samurai sword, bowed down, and handed it to Jack. He looked toward the ground out of respect to his master. Jack took the blade, pulled it from its scabbard, and looked it over. The blade was a marvelous work of craftsmanship. It was one solid piece of metal. The sword was very elegant and light. "What a beautiful blade, this is," Jack said. "I've heard that a samurai's sword is his soul." He then looked back at Tomodachi and added, "Too bad for you!"

Jack handed the blade to one of his polar bear brutes. The massive bear gripped the blade with both paws and snapped it in half.

"No!" Tomodachi shouted.

"Oh, don't fuss. The sword is the least of your worries. Think of it as the appetizer, and now it's time for the main course." Jack reached over and touched Yujin on the forehead. The necklace around his neck glowed a bright blue. Instantly, frost came forth from Jack's touch and encompassed Yujin in solid ice.

"Nooo!" Tomodachi shouted in agony. "I kill you! You pay!" The anger and hatred burned in Tomodachi's eyes.

"Next!" Jack shouted. The guards pushed Lotora forward. "Say goodbye to her, too!"

"Stop! Take me! Stop!" Tomodachi

yelled.

"Relax! I'm freeing her," answered Jack. He nodded his head, and the guards cut her ropes. "As agreed, you're free to go. Your daughter is waiting for you."

"Mommy! Mommy!" came the voice of a little raccoon cub that ran up to her mother. Lotora knelt down, hugged her, and cried. "Thank you! Oh, thank you!"

"See! I'm not without mercy," Jack announced.

Nero stood there with a dumbfounded look on his face. He could not understand why Jack would let her go free. Jack glared at his general. "What? You mean to tell me that you had no idea she was my spy? How do you think I always knew where they were?"

Tomodachi reacted strongly and shouted

at Lotora, "You! You did this? How could you? How could you?" Tomodachi struggled to break free from his fresh restraints, but it was no use.

Jack laughed as he watched Tomodachi struggle. "Face it, you can't win. Before long, the entire world will bow to me." Jack glanced over at his polar bear guards and shouted, "Take him away!"

Tomodachi's spirit had been broken, and his paws made weaponless. The loss of his daughter stole his will to live. A samurai now without honor, the only thing for him to look forward to was the grave. He felt like a fool for not realizing Lotora was a traitor, and it cost him his daughter's life. She was now eternally frozen. Nothing would ever be able to free her except Jack.

Nero and Jack's troops had rejoined each

other. Together they continued to Ursidea, which was still a long way off. Nero was speechless. He realized Jack was crafty, but he did not know the depths of what he had just witnessed. Deep down, he longed for Jack's power, authority, and throne. He had devised numerous plots to overthrow him, but had not found the right moment. He now realized that he was going to have to be much craftier than he anticipated. He even wondered if Jack suspected him of anything. Now, his devious plans would have to wait until Tomodachi's execution. Afterward, he could focus on his own ambitions.

They all trailed off together and left Lotora and her daughter behind. Honja remained hidden in her bag, with her book. Lotora at least had the decency to conceal Honja's presence from Jack. He never knew the little rabbit was there all along. In fact, nobody but Lotora knew. She sat down, held her daughter in her arms, and cried.

"What's wrong, Mommy?" asked the adorable little raccoon.

"I did something very bad, Sweetie. Something very bad," Lotora answered her daughter through a steady stream of tears.

"That's not true! You would never do something bad. You're the best mommy ever!" her daughter denied as they held each other tightly.

"Maybe there's a chance to make this right! If only I can reach this Santa person Flurry mentioned. Then, we could catch up with Jack before he reaches Ursidea," Lotora thought out loud. "Come on, Sweetie! We have a trip to make. I don't know where he is, but Flurry said that he would be in the north, so we go north."

Lotora pulled Honja from her bag and looked down at her daughter. "Can you hold on to him and keep him safe?"

"Yes, Mommy!" answered the little raccoon cub.

"Good. Now be careful with him." Lotora handed Honja to her daughter. Honja hated to be held, but at a time like this, he was in great need of comfort. Honja took refuge in the raccoon cub's arms. Lotora then led her daughter and Honja north.

Meanwhile, back near Ebongreene Forest, Flurry was on the move again. He rode on his reeyu while Nikolas and Katie traveled by horseback. Drift rode with one of the red pandas, and the other two red pandas went another direction to continue their task of recruiting more help.

Nikolas led the way. They were on a mission to find the elves and enlist them, also. Time was of the essence, and they rode hard and fast across the landscape.

It took them two full days to reach the land of the elves. The elves were spread out and quite diverse. Their people could be found in many different regions. These elves were the nearest to Ebongreene Forest. The trip there was full of hazards and dangers, but Flurry was with good company. Nikolas and Katie were very capable warriors, with Nick being a swordsman and Katie being an archer. As for Drift, he was the one and only teddy bear warrior to exist. Flurry had never seen nor heard of there ever being a teddy bear with such an occupation. Needless to say, Flurry was very impressed with Drift.

Their company spent a good deal of time

talking with the elves and negotiating. As Flurry looked on, he realized that he did not have what it took to be a diplomat. Flurry sat around bored and watched Nikolas, Katie, the red panda warrior, named Kadan, and the elves meet together. It must have ended well, since Flurry saw them all either shake hands or bow to one another.

Kringle came out of the meeting hall and approached Flurry. "Well, that's taken care of. Now we head north. I may still have some friends that way."

The elves had already taken care of saddling the horses and Flurry's reeyu. Flurry rushed up and petted her. "You know, I'm going to have to come up with a name for you. You've been so faithful. What should I call you?" Flurry rhetorically asked.

"Let's go!" shouted Nikolas.

"No! That's a terrible name!" answered Flurry. Nikolas looked confused by Flurry's response. At that moment Flurry realized that Nikolas was not answering his question, but was giving an order. Flurry giggled and said, "Oops! Hee hee hee hee hee!"

They rode north for a day and a half before they came across some fellow travelers. Nikolas raised his hand and signaled everyone to stop. There, in their path, was a familiar face.

"Lotora!" Flurry shouted. He hopped down from his ride and ran up to give her a hug.

"You're alive!" Lotora was ecstatic. "I thought you had died!"

"Nah, I'm fine."

"How? How did you survive?"

Flurry replied. "That's a long story. Oh! I

want you to meet someone special!" Flurry grabbed her by the paw and led her to Nikolas. "Do you know who this is?"

"No, but I really need to tell you something …" Lotora attempted to answer.

"It's Santa!" shouted Flurry.

"Oh! Are you Nikolas Kringle?" Lotora asked the man.

"Indeed I am, and you might be?" Nikolas inquired.

"Lotora! Her name is Lotora!" Flurry chimed in with a grin on his face.

"I have grave news and a confession. Tomodachi's daughter has been frozen in ice by Jack Frost. Tomodachi, himself, has been captured. He's going to be executed when they reach Ursidea. Jack wants to send a message to anyone who would dare defy him. And the worst news is that it's all my fault." Lotora collapsed to her knees and cried.

"Don't be so hard on yourself. These things happen," Nikolas replied.

"No, you don't understand. It's really my fault. I was secretly working for Jack. I communicated with him and told him our every move. I didn't want to. He made me do it. He told me that if I didn't, he would do something horrible to my daughter. To prove his resolve, he murdered my husband right in front of me. He then promised to return my daughter to me, unharmed, if I did what he said. But now, all hope is lost. Tomodachi's spirit is broken. He feels defeated, and Jack had his sword destroyed." Lotora gave quite the exposition about recent events, despite her shame.

Nikolas was upset, but had no idea what

to say. Kadan, the red panda, was very angry and wanted to apprehend her for justice, but Flurry changed the mood when he said, "It's okay. I forgive you." The cub ran over and hugged her. As he hugged her, he caught a glimpse of her daughter holding Honja.

"Honja!" Flurry shouted. He was so happy to see his friend. The teddy bear cub ran over, picked Honja up, and swung him around in the air before he gave him a hug. The rabbit covered his eyes. He feared getting sick from Flurry spinning him around. Honja hated every moment of what Flurry considered to be their adventure. The rabbit wanted their adventure to be over. It seemed like forever since they last saw their mother back in Middleasia.

Nikolas still did not know what to do about Lotora's betrayal, but he knew it was a matter better left for after they dealt with Jack. So he dropped the subject, for the time being, and brought her into the fold. Kadan voiced his vehement objections. Nikolas took the red panda's comments under advisement before he and his companions continued north. Kadan glared at Lotora the entire trip.

"Is there any valuable information you can give me about Jack, the number of soldiers with him, or his whereabouts?" Nikolas asked Lotora.

Lotora felt uneasy when she saw Kadan put a paw on his sword, but she tried to pretend that he was not there and focused on Nikolas. "He had what seemed like six thousand troops with him. I don't know why so many of them were with him. He must've been out conquering before he met up with us. Nero had about a dozen or so with him. However, what I think would be the most valuable information is that they're on foot, heading to Ursidea. They left me a little more than four days ago. They're also going the long way back. You can get there faster if you go north and come down around the other side of the lake."

Nikolas brought their group to a stop, got down from his horse, and unrolled a map. As he studied the terrain, he agreed that Lotora's route would get them to Ursidea before Jack. "Then we continue north!" Nikolas answered.

They made camp for the night. Kadan went hunting and brought back a deer for their meal. After dinner, it was time for bed. Honja already snored away, and Flurry was quickly nodding off when a paw came over his mouth. "Shhhhh! It's just me." Lotora whispered.

"Don't talk, just listen," Lotora continued. Flurry sat up and rubbed his eyes. "I'm giving this book to you." She pulled out *The Book of Snow* from her backpack. "I believe this should be yours. I want you to have it as a gift for the good you've done for us. Whatever happens, I feel that you deserve to have it."

Lotora walked back to her sleeping spot. She laid down and pulled her blanket up. Flurry was in awe, but he did not know what to think. It looked remarkably similar to the book he already had back home. Then Flurry had an idea. He grabbed a stone from the ground and carved his initials into the back cover of the book. "There," Flurry whispered to himself. "Now I'll be able to tell them apart when I bring this one home, too." Just then, the crystal glowed. "Stop it," Flurry ordered the crystal. "I said, stop it! Stop that. I mean it!" The gemstone continued to glow brightly. Flurry decided to pry the crystal from the book cover, and to his surprise, it came out with ease. He wrapped the crystal up and stuck it in the pouch that was given to him during his visit with the elves. Flurry stashed it away, fluffed his pillow, and drifted off to sleep.

Little did Flurry know that Nikolas was still awake and had observed the entire interaction. He believed everything was happening for a reason, and that Flurry was the key to it all. Only time would tell.

CHAPTER 7
URSIDEA

Orange flame ascended into the azure expanse. As if nature was not without a sense of irony, lustrous rays shot out across the lush terrain like flaming arrows. With the dawn came the hope of something new. However, the crimson rays were as though a harbinger of impending doom.

Typically the land was very beautiful: filled with flowers, gardens, and rivers. However, Jack's presence had turned the region cold and dreary. Snow now covered the ground as far as the eye could see.

Ursidea was a magnificent city. Before the days of Jack's rule, it was the hub for all of the different bear tribes and nations. It was a center for beauty and education. The neighboring nations viewed Ursidea as a beacon of hope and peace. The builders of the city did very little to ensure its protection. It was without walls or any other evident form of defense, for all were welcome to come or go as they pleased. Those days ended long ago.

Jack had ruled for so long, and was so powerful, that his pride led him to believe he had no need for the strong walls of his fortress, Ursadoom. He now lived in a palace, unmoved by any worry of threat. This very pride would be Jack's downfall, for he had no idea that his enemies planned to ambush him.

Jack's convoy approached the marvelous city with its marble structures and blue roofs. Thousands of polar bears were pleased to be back in a land where it was cold, as they were accustomed to. Nero was also glad to be done with the traveling. He looked forward to some much-needed rest and relaxation. As he pondered what he would do after Tomodachi's execution, the company came to a halt. Jack had raised his paw to indicate his command for the sudden stop.

Nero rode up next to him. "What is it, My Master?"

"Something's not right," the red panda answered. Jack shifted his gaze from side-to-side. He turned around and focused his attention on his prisoner. "You! Before your capture, how many did you successfully gather to your cause?" Tomodachi kept silent. The prisoner would not even acknowledge that he had been addressed.

"It's no use. With pride like that, he won't tell us anything," answered Nero. "Let me beat it out of him."

Jack was about to answer his general when something caught his attention. Jack spun around and looked out toward Ursidea again. "Something's wrong," Jack informed Nero. The red panda looked over at his warriors. "Everyone, have your weapons at the ready. We may be walking into a trap," he instructed them.

Jack gave the command to press forward. They continued cautiously down into the once lush but now snow-covered valley. When they came to the floor of the lowland, a man stood in their path. Jack knew this man well. Jack lowered himself from his mount and walked out to meet him.

"What are you doing here, Kringle?" Jack exclaimed with a hint of astonishment in his tone. Jack seemed impressed that Nikolas would even attempt such a brave move.

"I'm here to stop you. I'm putting an end to this, once and for all," Nikolas answered.

Jack was amused. He looked back at his army and then at Nikolas. "Fool! You're helplessly outnumbered, and my polar bears are ruthless. They'll rip anyone to shreds at my command. I suggest you step aside!" Jack ordered.

Nikolas pulled his sword from its scabbard. "I won't! I said it ends here, and I'm a man of my word." Nikolas whistled loudly, and the sound of horns bellowed in the distance. Without delay, riders on horseback surrounded the entire valley. From the ridge above, they held the tactical advantage.

Jack scoffed. "Ha! Elves? You really think I'm afraid of elves? If it's a fight you want, a fight you shall have!" Jack glanced at Nero and shouted, "Attack!"

Jack considered Nikolas to be inferior. He turned to walk away, but Nikolas grabbed him by the coat and threw him to the ground. "Oh, no you don't!" Nikolas pointed his sword at Jack. "Don't you dare turn your back on me! I said I came to finish this! Now, get up!" The red panda jumped back to his feet and armed himself.

The elves had been hiding in the city as well as surrounding the valley. Everyone rushed out for battle. Growling and roaring came from the polar bear army. The galloping of horses and clashing of swords echoed all around the valley of Ursidea. The battle was fierce, and the number of casualties had swiftly climbed in mere minutes.

Jack and Nikolas were locked in combat. They swung their swords at each other as they traded words. "Give up now! Your forces are already being defeated," Jack exclaimed.

"Never! I gave you the ability to live, and I can take it away!" Nikolas shouted back.

"No, you can't, actually. If you could, you would've done so long ago. I'm no fool!"

While in the midst of their fight, some polar bears decided to help their ruler and ran up to attack Nikolas. Katie quickly raised her bow and shot both of them with her arrows. "I've got your back," she shouted to Nikolas and winked.

"Awww, how cute. I'll be sure to make her suffer, too!" Jack threatened.

Jack's taunt enraged Nikolas. "You leave her alone!" He swung his sword wildly at the red panda. His unbridled emotion now gave Jack the advantage. The red panda slashed at Nikolas. The man had numerous wounds in a matter of minutes. Instead of being quick about it, however, Jack wanted to take his time in the man's execution. Jack enjoyed the suffering of others. The villain's pride gave him no reason for concern or urgency. Their conflict raged on. Katie took down any enemy who tried to interfere in the duel. Across the battlefield, Lotora, Flurry, and Honja had arrived. They rushed to Tomodachi's side.

They unbound the samurai, but Tomodachi refused to get up. He had lost the will to fight. He felt that he had lost his honor and deserved to die. Flurry tried to persuade him otherwise. "Come on! You have to try! Doggy told me that you're the one that defeats Jack." Flurry persuasively attempted to rouse the warrior.

"Yujin … gone. Sword … gone. Honor … gone." Tomodachi gazed despondently at the snow-covered ground he sat upon.

Lotora held out an object wrapped in cloth. "This is from Nikolas Kringle. He said the Great King told him to give it to you."

Tomodachi looked over at it. Lotora removed the cloth to reveal a beautiful sword. It was unlike any sword Tomodachi had used before. It was clearly not a samurai's weapon, but it was an elegant, double-edged beauty.

Tomodachi reached out and gripped the sword. To his surprise, it was much lighter than he expected it to be. "It's made from a blue star or by a blue star. I'm not really sure. Something like that, if I remember right," Flurry attempted to explain.

"No. Not work," Tomodachi replied and tossed the sword to the ground.

"You have to try!" Flurry insisted. "You haven't lost your honor yet. The battle isn't over. It isn't over until it's over. If not for yourself, do it for Yujin!" Flurry's words had an impact. Tomodachi's eyes glimmered. He took in a deep breath. Flurry sensed the spark revive in the warrior's spirit.

Tomodachi's facial expression firmed up,

and his paw gripped his new blade. "*Kawaii!* You right! Honor, or die! For Yujin!" Tomodachi stood up, took another deep breath, and looked over at Jack and Nikolas in their heated skirmish. "Stop, Jack!" Tomodachi shouted. He pointed at the evil red panda who slashed away at the wounded Kringle.

Tomodachi let out a war cry and ran into the battle. The samurai cut down every enemy in his path.

As he dueled Nikolas, Jack noticed Tomodachi headed straight toward them. In fact, the villain could see that the samurai had his fire back. Jack decided it was high time to retreat to his palace and let his army do the rest of the work for him. "Until next time," Jack addressed his human opponent, turned, and ran for his palace.

Flurry saw Jack's retreat and acted quickly. "Let's go! He's getting away! We have to stop him!"

"But how?" Lotora asked.

"I don't know yet. I'm making this up as I go. Come on!" Flurry shouted. He picked up his book and ran after Jack.

Being small, Flurry had a slight advantage of either going unnoticed or running under the legs of the horses and polar bears. As Flurry dashed across the battlefield, dark shadows covered the ground. Flurry looked up and saw the sky filled with reeyu. The red pandas from Ronin had arrived.

A horn sounded, and there were suddenly other warriors present at the battle. Flurry looked out across the land and saw a cat army, a squirrel army, wolves, bears, a massive army of lion-like creatures with horns, and many other types of beings he had never seen before. The lion-like animals reminded him of the Gargarins. The nations had arrived to unite against their common enemy.

The battlefield grew more intense. Flaming arrows flew through the air, and the clanging of swords resounded everywhere. Growls, howls, grunts, screams, and war cries were heard all over the place. Friend and foe alike dropped all around Flurry. It was chaos as he tried to navigate the battlefield to reach the palace. Lotora and Honja ran close behind him. Unfortunately, Nero saw them and decided to do something about it.

Flurry ran as fast as he could. He dodged flames, arrows, and falling creatures. He ran under legs, slid behind obstacles for cover, and managed to zigzag his way toward his destination.

The battle was currently out in the valley, but it drew closer to the city with each passing minute. Before long, the battle would be in the streets. Flurry ran as hard as he could, but it was not easy to also carry the book with him. He held it tightly to his chest with his arms crossed over it. Flurry, followed closely by Lotora and Honja, rushed through the city streets and cut across alleys to try and catch up with Jack.

"I have an idea," Lotora said. "You two go on, and I'll rejoin you later." Lotora ran off. Honja jumped on top of Flurry's head and held tightly to the cub's fur. Flurry edged up the side of a building, with his back to the wall. Polar bear guards patrolled the area. One guard was unaware that he had

THE BOOK OF SNOW

his back to Flurry, who stood only a few feet behind him.

Flurry scanned the area and saw Jack at the doors to his palace. "You! Come here!" Jack ordered the polar bear who presently towered over Flurry and Honja. The polar bear did as ordered. "Make sure nobody comes in here! Understood?"

"Yes, your Majesty," answered the guard. He was among eleven other guards who stood with their weapons ready. With a grand total of twelve polar bears, Flurry was uncertain how to get past them undetected.

Flurry tried to think up a plan, but it was too late. The next thing he saw was Lotora being marched out onto the street by Nero. The arctic fox called out to Flurry. "I know you're out there, cub! If you don't want me to kill your friend, come out from your

J.S. SKYE

hiding place!"

Flurry turned to Honja. "Stay here and hide. He has never seen you before. You'll be safe here." Honja had a tear in his eye. The bunny hugged Flurry goodbye. Honja felt that despite their differences, it was touching that Flurry cared so much about him to try and conceal him from danger.

"Here I am! I'm coming out!" shouted Flurry. He walked out into the open area in front of Jack's palace. His arms were still wrapped around the book.

"Very noble of you, cub!" Nero ridiculed Flurry's brave decision. "Guards! Apprehend these two!" Nero ordered.

"We can't. We're on strict orders to guard this palace," answered the highest ranking of the polar bear soldiers.

"I'm your general, and I said ..." Nero

began.

"It doesn't matter. The order came directly from Jack," the polar bear replied.

"Very well! I'll take them in myself!" Nero pulled his sword and pointed it at Lotora. "Both of you walk, or this raccoon gets it first." Flurry and Lotora walked up the steps to the palace. The guards opened the doors and let them in.

Nero led them down a hallway and into the throne room. "Your Majesty, I caught these two trying to catch up to you. I can only assume they planned to harm you," Nero informed his master while down on one knee.

Jack turned and saw Lotora and Flurry. At the sight of Flurry, Jack became furious. "Him! Where did HE come from? He's responsible for what happened at ..." Jack stopped mid thought. Then, as if he had been enlightened, he said, "Wait a minute! Is this rebellion your doing?"

Jack's face twitched. He stopped to take a breath, but clenched his teeth and made fists with his paws. He placed one paw on his sword and darted down the steps toward Flurry and Lotora. "You've done well, Nero! Now leave us!" Jack instructed his general. Nero bowed and stepped out of the room.

"Do you know how much trouble you've caused me, little one?" Jack addressed the teddy bear cub. "Answer me!" Flurry was startled. He looked up and noticed that Jack did not have any scars on his face. Flurry clearly remembered that Jack had three scars down his right eye, but they were not there. *This must be a younger Jack*, he thought to himself. *That's why Jack knew who I was when we met in the cave.* It was all starting to come together in Flurry's mind.

Flurry sarcastically replied, "Uhmmm, no. What did I do? Did I give you a hug? Probably not, because you seem like you really need one. Oh, I bet it's because I'm cuter than you! Is that it? I bet that's it!"

Flurry's words infuriated Jack. He pulled his sword, raised it above his head, and was about to strike Flurry down when a shout came. "Stop!" Jack looked up and saw Tomodachi. The warrior stood in Jack's throne room, sword drawn.

"How did you get in here? I had this place heavily guarded," Jack growled at the samurai.

"Those twelve? Ha!" Tomodachi replied. "They … died well."

Jack shoved Flurry and Lotora out of the way and ran toward Tomodachi. "Ahhh!" Jack screamed. "This ends here!"

As Jack drew near to Tomodachi, the samurai's new sword glowed a bright, radiant blue. Their blades met, and their duel commenced.

Flurry rushed over to Lotora and helped her up. "Quick! We need to do something," Flurry insisted.

"What? We aren't warriors," Lotora replied.

"Hmmm, that pedestal looks a lot like the one that I found this on." Flurry pulled the glowing blue gemstone from his pouch.

"You took it out of the book? Why did you do that?" Lotora exclaimed. She was clearly upset.

"It wouldn't stop glowing. I had to do that

so I could get some sleep," Flurry replied. "What would happen if I put this thing up on that pedestal?"

"That's Jack's source for turning people into ice. It would probably freeze you," Lotora theorized.

"Nah! The cold never bothers me," Flurry replied. He was so sure of himself.

Meanwhile, Tomodachi and Jack's battle raged on. Tomodachi was so fierce that anyone would have feared him. He was a force to be reckoned with. Jack struck Tomodachi in the face and pulled the samurai's sword down for another blow, but Tomodachi struck first and raked his claws down Jack's face.

"Ahhhhh!" Jack screamed in agony. The villain took his paw away from his right eye to return to their fight. Tomodachi had left his mark. Three claw wounds marred Jack's face. "You'll pay for that!" Jack shouted and viciously swung his sword at Tomodachi.

Flurry attempted to place the stone on the pedestal, but Nero and some guards had arrived and attempted to grab him. Flurry tossed the stone to Lotora. "Catch!" Flurry shouted. The guard grabbed Flurry, but it was too late. Lotora now had the stone.

Lotora ran across the room to evade the arctic foxes, but she was cornered. They closed in on her from two sides as Flurry was held by another guard.

Out of desperation, Lotora threw the stone. It landed on the ground and rolled up to one of the pillars that encircled the throne room. "Grab it! Honja, grab it!" she shouted.

Behind the pillar a little rabbit stood. He had snuck into the palace. He looked at the gemstone and back at Lotora, then at the gemstone and up at Flurry. His legs shook, and his mouth quivered with fear.

Nero saw Honja and shouted to the guard that held Flurry, "Take care of that mouse!"

Suddenly, Honja was outraged. In his own language, he thought to himself, *A mouse? A mouse? Who does he think he is?* Honja ran as fast as he could straight at Nero, head-butted him in the leg, and bit him. Nero screamed in pain and shouted, "Someone kill that rodent!"

Honja then made a dash for the gemstone. He picked it up in his mouth, and its color changed from blue to red. Honja rushed off with the stone. The guards chased him around the room. They leapt at him and dove into his path. Honja was so small and nimble that none of the guards could catch him. He weaved in and out of his obstacles with ease.

Flurry was now free and glimpsed Jack advancing on Tomodachi. Flurry needed to think fast. "Say goodbye," Jack snarled at Tomodachi and raised his sword to strike.

"Okay, goodbye!" came a small voice from across the throne room as a stone struck Jack in the head. The blow caused him to drop his sword and collapse to the ground.

Tomodachi looked over at Flurry, and for the first time had a genuine smile. He nodded with gratitude. Tomodachi jumped to his feet with his sword in paw. Jack struggled to get back up, dazed from Flurry's attack. Tomodachi resumed the duel. Jack pulled himself together enough to block Tomodachi's strike. Their battle raged on, and Flurry now turned his attention back to Honja.

Flurry ran back up to the pedestal. One of the guards had fallen nearby, and Flurry knew he could use the guard as a footstool to reach the pedestal. Flurry shouted to his friend. "Honja, throw it here!"

Jack and Tomodachi were still in a sweltering battle a few feet in front of the throne. Honja leapt over a fallen guard and tossed the gemstone to his friend. Flurry caught the stone. In an instance the bear cup jumped from the prostrate fox and over to the pedestal. The cub hung on with one paw, and with the other he placed the stone on the pedestal's surface.

Suddenly, a thunderous sound shook the palace walls. Jack and Tomodachi paused to see what Flurry had done. Tomodachi took a few steps back from his opponent. A shockwave burst forth from the crystal, which threw Flurry across the room and knocked everyone else to the ground. A beam of blue light bolted out from the gemstone, struck Jack, and flung him straight into the throne. The red panda was instantly frozen in place. Ice formed all around the throne so quickly that it took place in the blink of an eye. It narrowly missed Tomodachi.

"No!" shouted Nero. He ran up to the pedestal and reached out to grab the gemstone. A flash of energy emitted from the crystal and instantly turned Nero into a pillar of ice.

The room fell silent. The guards realized that Jack and Nero were beyond saving and would remain frozen forever. Tomodachi's blade no longer glowed. The samurai turned toward the arctic foxes and advanced on their position. In fear they laid down their weapons and surrendered to the red panda warrior.

Lotora was shocked at what she had witnessed. She came up to Flurry and asked, "How did you know?"

"Well, I found a crystal just like that one in a cave once. It was on a thing like that one there. When I took it, Jack got free. So I thought that maybe it would work the other way around," Flurry replied.

Lotora's chin quivered in fear as she turned to Tomodachi. The raccoon bowed her head and cried. "I'm so sorry for what I've done. Jack murdered my husband and held my daughter captive. I'm truly sorry, and I vow to do everything in my power to find a way to free Yujin from Jack's curse."

Tomodachi huffed at her words. The samurai turned away from Lotora and promptly marched out of the throne room. Outside the battle raged on. The fighting had spread into streets of the city. Ursidea was in ruins. Jack's forces were diminished significantly. Tomodachi exited the palace, looked around, and called back for one of his prisoners inside. An arctic fox rushed out the palace entryway and up to the samurai. "Use horn! Stop fight!" Tomodachi ordered.

The fox pulled out his horn and blew loudly. The call announced their defeat. The other warriors ceased their advance. Nikolas and Katie, when they heard the horn sound, looked at each other with amazement. "Could it be true?" Nikolas asked. "Help me up, please."

Katie brought Nikolas to his feet. He looked out over the battleground. Nikolas saw many casualties, but he also saw victory over Jack's forces. He could not believe his eyes. So many things could have gone wrong, and their numbers were initially inferior to Jack's.

He continued to scan the battlefield, and saw a little white bear cub run across the grass toward him. "Santa! Santa! We won! Jack and Nero are both gone!" Flurry shouted with much enthusiasm. Nikolas could hardly fathom what he heard. Could it be so? This was the best news in many years. There would finally be peace.

Later that night, there were grand celebrations all over the different regions Jack had once ruled. Fireworks exploded in the air. The streets and forests were filled with singing and dancing. It was the merriest of occasions. In fact, it was the biggest party Flurry had ever seen. His favorite part was all of the food. It was a royal feast that he could enjoy while he listened to the wonderful music and partook in all of the various forms of entertainment the night had to offer.

Over the course of the following days, the different kingdoms met together and came to a consensus to demolish the entire city of Ursidea. They would take the stone and rubble to bury the throne room and pack it all in with dirt, so that it would no longer be remembered. This marked a new beginning for them all.

In Ebongreene Forest, Nikolas and Katie stood tall and were immeasurably proud of Flurry and Honja. Flurry told them that

Honja was the true hero, which resulted in the little rabbit receiving a lot of wonderful treats to munch on. Honja was happy it was all over, but his thoughts were elsewhere. The bunny longed for his home.

"Now, it's time to rebuild and to focus on cultivating peace," Nikolas said to Katie.

"Since this is a new era for everyone, maybe you should start going by Christopher instead of Nick," Katie teased the young man.

"You know I hate that name, Katie!" Nikolas retorted.

"Hmmm, I kind of like it," she replied, and kissed him on the cheek. Nikolas blushed.

"Very well, I'll do it if you go by Catherine from now on, too." Katie laughed without providing him with an answer.

Honja and Flurry had wandered away from the crowd, and both sat beside a little brook. Honja enjoyed a carrot while Flurry pondered what to do next. He wanted to go home, but he had no idea how to do that.

Drift came up and sat next to him. "Well, you did it again. Great job!" said Drift.

"Again?" Flurry asked. "Did what again?"

"Oh, uh … never mind," answered Drift.

"What will the teddy bears do now?"

"I suppose we'll try to find a new place to call home. I've always wanted to build my own home and settle down. Maybe have a cub or two of my own."

"You should try the north. It's a great place. I love it!"

"Noted. I'll definitely keep that in mind," Drift commented.

At this time, Lotora walked up to join them. "Flurry, I have bad news," the raccoon spoke with anguish in her tone. "Since you traveled here by the book, you can no longer get back by the book, because you removed the crystal. The book is powerless now."

Flurry felt tremendous grief and did not know what to say. Honja looked even sadder. Flurry's reeyu, who stood by, came up and licked him. "Awww, I wish I could get back home and bring you with me, but the book isn't working, see?" Flurry demonstrated by touching a page in the book. Instantly Flurry, Honja, and the reeyu vanished. The book slammed shut on its own, and the clasp locked.

Drift and Lotora were both startled by what they saw. They shouted for Nikolas, and he rushed over. "What happened to

Flurry?" Lotora asked the man.

Nikolas smiled and replied, "He's home now."

"What do we do with the book?"

"Give it to me. I'll keep it safe and give it back to him at another time."

Lotora got up and handed Nikolas the book. "Well, I need to head over to Ursidea, what's left of it. They've already relocated Nero and plan to put a plaque on the pedestal as a warning for generations to come. They asked for my direction on the matter. Thank you for all you've done, Nikolas."

Nikolas and Lotora exchanged hugs. As she prepared to leave, he said to her, "Good luck, take care of your daughter, and you can call me Christopher from now on." Lotora smiled and nodded.

She shook paws and hugged the others. When she turned around, she saw Tomodachi standing in her path. Fear overtook her. She was surprised when he bowed to her. She bowed back. Drift looked to the samurai and said, "You just missed Flurry. He's gone back home now."

"Not miss. Remember," answered Tomodachi. He then walked down the hill, mounted his reeyu, and flew off into the sunrise of a new era.

Back in Middleasia, the sky was pitch black. The town slept peacefully. Most of the houses were unlit and silent. However, one home was an exception.

Boaz glanced toward Noah and asked, "What are we going to do? Flurry and Honja are inside the book!" Boaz had a look of sheer terror on his face. Noah shrugged.

Caboose had already gotten out of bed and now sniffed at the book. The polar bear dragged the book back out from under Flurry's bed.

"Maybe we should open it and see if say are in sare," lisped Caboose.

"No way! What if we open it, and we get sucked in, too?" Boaz replied. "I don't know how we're going to break the news to Mommy. We need to talk to the person Flurry calls Santa. Maybe he'll know what to do."

"I'm going to try it," said Caboose. With his mouth he pulled on the locked clasp and pushed on the book with his front paws.

"Caboose, no!" shouted Boaz.

Suddenly the book sprang open, and blue light radiated from its pages. Flurry, Honja, and a baby reeyu came forth. The book slammed shut and locked again.

Boaz's mouth dropped open. "Uh, what just happened?"

"Oh, hello!" Flurry giggled.

Honja was so delighted that he hopped up and down and danced back and forth before he realized that they all stared at him in disbelief. He quickly sat down and crossed his arms.

Laughter broke out, and everyone hugged each other. "I feel like it has been a month since I've seen any of you!" Flurry exclaimed. "I missed all of you very much, and Mommy, too! Where is she?"

"Flurry, be quiet!" Boaz exclaimed. "Mommy and Daddy are still in bed sleeping."

"Not anymore!" came a voice from the door.

"Mommy!" Flurry shouted. The cub rushed over to her and hugged her leg. Honja did likewise.

"What has gotten into you two?"

"You wouldn't believe us if we told you," Flurry replied.

Lynn looked over at what she deduced to be a baby dragon on the floor, and then back at her boys. She smiled and said, "Try me."

EPILOGUE
FAITHFUL AND TRUE

After Flurry's return to Middleasia, he told his mother the entire story of his adventures with Honja, Lotora, Tomodachi, and Yujin. To his surprise, she believed him. Flurry then got her permission to take his baby reeyu to his home in Ursus, so someone could take care of her for him while he was in Middleasia. His mother agreed, and Flurry made the trip.

While in Ursus, Flurry contacted a friend whom he thought might be the most appreciative of an infant reeyu. While he waited for his reeyu's new caretaker to arrive, Flurry sat in Christopher Kringle's comfy chair by the fireplace and ate some of Catherine's chocolate chip cookies.

Christopher had been out for a while, but was now returning home. He was amused to find the little cub in such a big chair. "Well, hello there," came Christopher's greeting.

"Hello, Santa!" Flurry replied with cookie crumbs on his scarf and chocolate all around his mouth.

Christopher chuckled at the sight. He took off his coat, hung it up, and then sank into a seat across the table from Flurry. "I heard that you have yourself a baby reeyu out there."

"Uh huh!" Flurry replied, while he stuffed his mouth with another cookie.

"Where did you get it?" Christopher asked.

"Oh, come on! You know," Flurry replied. His concentration did not break from the cookies for even a moment. Christopher was amused by the cub's response. Flurry then added, "I do have one question. The day I was born, did you know that it was me?"

Christopher chuckled and winked at the bear cub. "Well now, I can't reveal all of my secrets. But for you … let's just say that I had a hunch. Why else would I have given you that book?" After a brief pause, a grin came to Christopher's face. He remarked, "You know, it does have your initials on the back, after all."

Flurry looked up at the man, surprised, and grinned nervously. Christopher broke the tension by laughing, and Flurry joined in. Their laughter was interrupted by a knock at the door. Catherine opened the door to reveal a red panda.

"Chingu!" Flurry shouted. He jumped down from the chair and ran over to give him a hug. "I'll show you what I have for you. I think you'll love it."

Flurry led Chingu by the paw to a barn. As they entered, there sat a purple-colored reeyu infant. Chingu's eyes widened with delight. He did not have a reeyu of his own. Most of his older brothers did, but he never had the privilege. He looked back at Flurry and nodded with approval.

"I thought you would be the perfect match for her, but when I come to visit, I get first dibs on a ride." Flurry's comment was met with a small grin. "Oh yeah, I almost forgot!

Her name is Faith!"

*****

Back in the past, Lotora stood in the ruins of Ursidea to oversee the final work on burying the city. They created a warning plaque to put on the pedestal to prevent anyone from touching it and suffering Jack's fate. The crystal glowed with brilliant yellow light.

Another raccoon approached her. He was elderly and wore bifocals. He carried a number of books and scrolls. He set his items down on a table and pulled a thin, metal plate from the bag at his side.

"Here it is!" he said. "I shall read it to you. 'Frozen in time, Frost will keep. Deep underground, Jack will sleep. By the origin paw, may the ice be moved. If so you do, all will be doomed. Beautiful and lovely, the gem may be. Remove it and find trouble indeed.' What do you think?"

Lotora stood there and thought about it for a moment. Then she replied. "Well, it's already done, so go ahead and attach it to the pedestal. However, I think we should add something more down below it."

"Okay," said the elderly raccoon. "I have my chisel set with me. Let me write it down. What else do you want to add?"

Lotora said, "Add the phrase, 'Flurry, don't even think about it!'"

ABOUT J.S. SKYE

J.S. Skye grew up in the Midwestern region of the United States. At a very young age, it was apparent that he was very talented. Finding that he was gifted in music and art, he plunged himself into both. As time passed, he set aside music to focus even more of his attention on developing his skills as an illustrator.

All throughout his years in school, J.S. Skye spent every available moment creating and developing fictional worlds. Caring about realism, he developed multiple people groups, countries, worlds, and even languages. His fictional realms were created through both written and visual mediums.

After traveling to almost a dozen different countries and studying different cultures, J.S. Skye decided to implement his interests in ancient cultures, history, languages, mythology, and more into his writings. He decided it was best to pour his heart and passion into writing instead of having divided interests between both art and literature.

J.S. Skye has accumulated a fairly large collection of his various writings. These stories range from all types of different genres such as mystery, science fiction, fantasy, and even horror. Friends encouraged the aspiring writer to produce a novel and see how things progressed from there.

J.S. Skye's first novel, *The Granted Wish*, was met with cheerful affirmation. The positive feedback was overwhelming and unexpected. Fans of his *Flurry the Bear* novels grew and began to clamor for more. From this point forward, his first novel series came to be.

For more information or to get in touch with J.S. Skye personally, he may be contacted by e-mail at:

JS-Skye@FlurryTheBear.com

ALSO BY J.S. SKYE

Flurry the Bear – The Granted Wish

Flurry the Bear – The Land of the Sourpie

Flurry the Bear – The Throne of Frost

Flurry the Bear – The Rising Tide

www.ingramcontent.com/pod-product-compliance
Lightning Source LLC
Chambersburg PA
CBHW030305180626
46810CB00003B/918